RANGER CREED

BROTHERHOOD PROTECTORS

NEW YORK TIMES BESTSELLING AUTHOR
ELLE JAMES

EBOOK ISBN: 978-1-62695-273-7

PRINT ISBN: 978-1-62695-274-4

Dedicated to my father, a gentle man who taught me the value of hard work and persistence. I miss him every day.
Elle James

AUTHOR'S NOTE

Visit ellejames.com for titles and release dates
and join Elle James's Newsletter

CHAPTER 1

"RUNNING BEAR, YOU COPY?" Christina Samson, sitting at dispatch, asked.

Lani Running Bear keyed the mic on her radio. "I copy."

"We just received a call from Mattie Lightfoot. She needs you out at her place on Willow Creek ASAP."

Lani sighed. On her thirteenth hour of a twelve-hour shift, she was tired and ready to call it a night. Or, in this case, a morning. "Roger," she said, and turned her Blackfeet Law Enforcement Service vehicle around in the middle of the road and headed back the direction she'd come while on her way in for shift change.

Mattie Lightfoot lived in a mobile home next to Willow Creek with her grandson, Tyler. She'd raised Tyler since he was four years old, when his mother left the reservation to go make her fortune in Vegas. Her daughter, Stella Lightfoot, hadn't known who Tyler's father was. None of the men she'd slept with claimed him. Mattie's daughter had promised to send for Tyler when she'd made enough money to support them both.

Stella never sent for Tyler. She never came back to visit her son and, after a couple of years, she quit calling.

Mattie did what she could for Tyler. She worked at a convenience store in Browning, bringing in just enough money to pay utilities and groceries. Food stamps and food pantries had become a necessity. She made sure Tyler had food, even when she didn't.

A fiercely proud Blackfeet matriarch, Mattie was a respected member of the tribe. When she called for help, it was something very serious.

Lani could have refused the call and let the tribal police officer from the next shift take it. But, when she'd sworn in, she'd promised to respect and look out for members of her tribe, her family.

The drive to Mattie's place took fifteen minutes, traveling on a number of different gravel roads, until Lani finally turned onto the rutted path leading to Mattie's single-wide mobile home.

Several vehicles were parked in the yard next to Mattie's old red and white Ford pickup with the rusted wheel wells and bald tires.

Recognizing the new charcoal gray Denali, a full-sized SUV belonging to tribal elder Raymond Swift-water, Lani tensed. In her opinion, Swiftwater was a pompous ass, full of his own self-importance. He liked to think he could make decisions for the entire tribe without consulting the other elders. And he bullied the others who were older and wiser than he was into agreeing with his way of thinking.

The man was accompanied by Stanley and Stewart Spotted Dog, his minions and the muscle he kept close for intimidation purposes. Stan and Stew had broad shoulders and thick necks and arms. They were effective visual deterrents, and strong enough to take down anyone who bothered their boss.

Swiftwater crossed his arms over his chest. "About time tribal police showed up."

Lani ignored the man and walked toward the trailer. "Where's Mattie?"

"Inside," Ray said. "It ain't good. Sure you have the stomach for it?"

Since she didn't know what *it* was, she couldn't say. Instead, she walked past Swiftwater, climbed the rickety stairs and knocked on the door. "Mattie, it's me, Lani Running Bear."

A woman's sob sounded from inside. "He's gone. My boy is gone."

Lani frowned, her chest constricting at the despair in the older woman's voice. "Mattie, may I come in?"

"Door's open," Mattie said, her voice muffled.

Lani entered through the narrow door into the dark interior of a mobile home that had seen more moons than Lani had been on this earth.

Mattie Lightfoot was on the floor beside the inert body of her grandson, Tyler. He lay on his back, his face smashed, his arms battered, his chest and belly slashed by what appeared to be multiple knife wounds.

Lani's chest tightened. She'd liked the kid. He'd been going somewhere. Tyler had been committed to completing his degree and getting on with his life as soon as he could. But mostly, he'd been kind to everyone and never had anything bad to say about anyone, Native American or otherwise.

Mattie stroked Tyler's long, thick, black hair back from his forehead, tears streaming down her face as she rocked back and forth. "He's gone."

Lani didn't have to touch the base of his throat to know she'd find no pulse, but she did anyway. As she suspected, his skin was already cool to the touch, and no amount of searching would produce a pulse. "What happened, Mattie?" she asked softly.

Mattie closed her eyes and rocked. "I don't know. I don't know who could have done this to my Tyler."

Lani hated asking questions of the woman when she was deeply distressed. But she had to know as much as possible to help find who'd beaten the poor kid to death. "Did you find him here? Or did someone bring him here like this?"

"He was here when I came home from work," Mattie said. "I should have been here for him. Maybe none of this would have happened. If I'd been home, he wouldn't be dead."

"You don't know that. You could have been hurt as well."

"Rather me than him," Mattie said. "He had so much to live for."

Lani glanced around the interior of the single-wide mobile home. Though it was old, Mattie kept it clean. A mismatch of dishes was stacked neatly on a drainboard by the sink. Laundry lay neatly folded on the built-in couch. There was no blood pooling beneath Tyler's body, nor was there any broken glass or furniture in the vicinity of the body. The young man had been beaten and stabbed multiple times.

The crime hadn't been committed inside the trailer, which meant whoever had killed him had brought him there.

"Did you see anyone leaving your yard?"

Again, Mattie shook her head. "No one was here when I got home, and I didn't pass anyone on the road coming in." She stared at her grandson. "Who would have done this to Tyler? He was such a good boy."

"I'm sorry, Mattie. I don't know who did this, but I will find out. We'll find who did this to Tyler." She hoped she wasn't lying. Too often, crimes on the rez remained unsolved. "Mattie, the FBI will be involved

5

in solving this crime. They have a lot of resources at their disposal that our own tribal police don't. They'll likely perform an autopsy and determine what weapons were used and what was the actual time of Tyler's death."

"Good. I want you to use whatever means possible to find Tyler's killer and bring him to justice."

Lani nodded. "When was the last time you saw Tyler...alive?"

Mattie's eyes filled with tears. "Yesterday afternoon. I had the night shift at the convenience store."

"Was he planning on going anywhere after dinner? Meeting anyone?"

She gave a hint of a smile. "He was going to see Natalie Preston, his girlfriend in Conrad. They had a date. He was going to take her out to the new diner for supper. He'd been working extra hours at the K Bar L Ranch so he could treat her to something special."

"Do you know if he made it to Natalie's?"

Mattie shook her head. "I had to work. I was looking forward to hearing all about their date." More tears slipped down the older woman's face.

Lani reached for Mattie's hand, squeezed it, and then pushed to her feet. "Did you call Raymond Swiftwater after you called the police?"

Mattie shook her head. "I didn't. He showed up a few minutes before you."

Lani's jaw tightened.

Swiftwater was known for showing up at reservation crime scenes.

"Could you make them leave?" Mattie asked, looking up at her.

Lani's lips pressed together in a thin line. "I'll do my best. In the meantime, I need to make some calls back at the station. I'll be back. Try not to disturb Tyler's body or any evidence. The FBI will want to look over everything very closely."

Mattie nodded and continued to stroke Tyler's hair, despite having been told not to disturb Tyler's body.

Lani left the trailer. As she descended the steps to the ground, Swiftwater approached her.

"So, what do you think?"

"I don't know what to think. A thorough investigation will have to be conducted."

"One of our people is dead," Swiftwater said. "What are you going to do about it?"

Lani squared her shoulders. "I'm going to do what I'm paid to do, and that is to investigate and find out who killed him. Now, if you'll excuse me, I need to get the FBI out here."

When she tried to go around Swiftwater, he stepped in her way, blocking her path. "Why must you call the FBI? This happened on the reservation."

"You know perfectly well the FBI has responsibility for investigating murders on the reservation."

She lifted her chin. "You know we don't have the training or the resources to conduct a thorough investigation within Blackfeet Law Enforcement Service."

Swiftwater sneered. "Then what are you good for? Writing speeding tickets and giving rides home to drunks?"

"As you are also aware, we don't have the ability to perform autopsies. We need to know the cause of death and time of death."

"I can tell you how he died," Swiftwater said. "A white man crossed onto the reservation and killed Tyler Lightfoot."

Lani planted her fists on her hips. "And you know that how? Were you there? Did you see it happen? And if you were there and saw it happen, why didn't you do something to stop it, or at least call it in?"

Swiftwater's face turned a ruddy red beneath his naturally dark skin. "We don't need an autopsy to determine what happened. It's obvious. Tyler dared to date one of their own. White men don't like it when Blackfeet date their women. Check with his girlfriend's family. I bet you'll find the murderer there."

"We'll get the FBI involved to help us find the murderer."

Swiftwater shook his head. "We don't like the FBI crawling around the reservation."

She drew a deep breath, trying to hold onto her

temper. "We don't have access to the resources available within the FBI. They have the resources and skills needed to solve this kind of crime."

Swiftwater's eyes narrowed. "And how often do they solve crimes on the reservation? I don't know why they can't leave it to our own people to solve the crimes."

Lani frowned. "You know we're always short-handed. We barely have enough staff to man two shifts."

"I've offered my own men as contract labor to help with law enforcement efforts."

She wouldn't trust Swiftwater's men any more than she'd trust Swiftwater. She suspected they were all corrupt; she just didn't have the evidence to prove it. "They aren't certified police officers. They have no authority to enforce the laws."

Lani was tired of his harassment. She narrowed her eyes. "Do you know anything about Tyler's death?"

Swiftwater blinked. "No."

"Then how did you come to be here so quickly?" she asked.

The tribal elder lifted his chin. "As a tribal elder, I have access to the police scanner. As a man responsible for the welfare of his tribe, I like to know what's happening. I also like to know how fast our law enforcement officers respond in situations such as this."

Lani snorted and turned away.

"I will report to the tribal elders how long it took you to arrive on scene."

Not bothering to reply, Lani climbed into her service vehicle, requested assistance and asked dispatch to notify the FBI.

Lani returned to the trailer to wait with Mattie. While they waited, Lani used her cellphone to take pictures of the crime scene, Tyler's body and the many wounds that had been inflicted. She knew the FBI would conduct a thorough investigation but wasn't sure they would share the information with her.

Within the hour, many of Mattie's friends and tribe women arrived in support of Mattie. At the same time, the tribal elders arrived and formed a circle around Swiftwater.

Lani, with Mattie in tow, exited the mobile home, wanting to know what the elders were discussing, and needing the older woman out of the trailer when the women converged on her. They didn't need to contaminate the crime scene any more than Mattie already had.

She found out soon enough.

"Officer Running Bear," Chief Hunting Horse called out.

Lani stepped forward. "Yes, sir."

"As the FBI will be involved in this investigation,

we want Police Chief Black Knife to be their contact. No others."

"That means you are officially off this case," Swiftwater said, stepping forward to stand beside Chief Hunting Horse.

At that moment, the chief of tribal police arrived.

Swiftwater nodded toward his vehicle. "Officer Running Bear, you can leave now."

Lani ignored Swiftwater and converged upon her head of law enforcement, Police Chief Black Knife. "Are you going to let the elders pull rank on you?"

Her boss frowned. "What are you talking about?"

"They just pulled me off this murder case."

He frowned. "What did they say?"

"That you will be the direct contact with the FBI investigation."

His frown deepened. "I'll find out what's going on." He left her standing by his vehicle and joined the tribal elders. A few minutes later, he returned, a scowl marring his forehead. "You're officially off the case."

"What? Why?" she asked.

Black Knife's face was set in stone. "There'll be no discussion. I'll see you back at the station."

When she opened her mouth to protest, he held up his hand. "No discussion."

Anger burned through her. She glanced toward the front of the mobile home where Mattie Lightfoot was being led away from the crime scene by Swiftwater.

Her gaze met Mattie's distraught one. The woman looked to her as if asking what was happening.

Lani started toward her.

A hand on her arm stopped her.

"You're off the case," Police Chief Black Knife reminded her.

"I just want to help Mattie."

"Go home. Your shift has ended." The stern look he gave her ended her arguments.

She wanted to go to Mattie and reassure her that she'd do everything in her power to find her grandson's killer, but she couldn't.

Maybe she couldn't do anything in an official capacity, but she could do something in an unofficial capacity, and she had an idea of who she could get to help her.

Lani took her service vehicle back to the station, climbed into her Jeep and headed to her cottage at the edge of the reservation. She hadn't gone five miles along the road home before a massive lump in the road forced her to slow to a complete stop.

She stared at the lump for a moment before her heart dropped to the pit of her belly. She pulled her service weapon out of her shoulder holster and stepped out of her vehicle, searching the roadside and ditches for any sign of movement. Nothing moved, including the lump in front of her.

She knew before she reached it what it was. The question wasn't so much what it was, but who.

Dressed in a gray hooded sweatshirt and sweat-pants, the victim lay on one side, facing away from Lani. Her police training had her estimating height and weight. Based on how long the body was, it was either a man or a very tall woman.

As she rounded the body, she gasped. The man's face had been so badly beaten that she couldn't tell who it was. And just like Tyler, he'd been stabbed multiple times in the chest and abdomen.

Lani checked for a pulse. For a long moment, she rested her fingers on his battered neck, hoping she might find a pulse. When she finally gave up, she started to pull her hand away.

The man's body jerked, his hand came out and grabbed her wrist.

Shocked, Lani tried to pull away, but his grip was so strong, she couldn't break free.

The man's eyes opened, and he stared at her through quickly swelling eyes, his pupils dilated. "Hep ma," he groaned.

Lani forced herself to calm. The man was still alive, but for how long? "Who did this to you?"

The man made a sound like a hiss then collapsed back to the ground. His grip relaxed on her wrist, his hand falling to the ground.

Lani checked again for a pulse. Nothing. She

searched his pockets for some form of identification but found none.

She hurried back to her SUV, pulled out her handheld radio and called dispatch. "Need an ambulance ASAP." She gave the location and information on the victim. Within minutes, the Blackfeet Emergency Medical Service arrived.

They were unable to revive the victim before loading him into the ambulance.

By that time, Police Chief Black Knife arrived, along with Swiftwater and his minions.

The chief listened to her account and made notes. When she'd finished, he tipped his head toward her SUV. "You can go now."

"Sir, with all due respect, I need to be there when the FBI does their investigation."

He shook his head. "You heard the elders. I'll be the only contact for this investigation. You're off duty. Go get some rest."

Lani snorted. "Two bodies in less than twenty-four hours. You think I'm going to rest? Do you even know who that man is?"

He nodded. "It was Ben Wolf Paw."

"Ben?" Lani's heart contracted. "Ben's one of the nicest guys on the reservation. Why?"

"I don't know, but we'll figure it out." He gripped her arm. "In the meantime, I need you to take a few days off."

She frowned. "Are you kidding me? Why?

"This has been a lot for you."

She frowned. What the hell was going on? Why were they freezing her out? "I've seen worse in Afghanistan. You can't put me on leave."

"I can, and I will." He gave her stern look. "Take the leave, or I'll have to fire you." He turned and left, not giving her an opportunity to argue.

Lani stood for a long moment after the ambulance left and everyone else cleared out. She stared at the place Ben had been lying on the road.

No blood. He'd been dumped after he'd been beaten and stabbed. Had he been murdered in the same location as Tyler, and then dumped here?

She didn't have the answers and, if the police chief had his way, she wouldn't get them.

Bullshit on that. She couldn't take a few days off and not do anything. Someone was killing good people on the reservation. And she intended to keep her promise to Mattie. These murders would not be left like so many on the reservation—unsolved. Not when she could do something about it.

As soon as she reached her cottage, she called an acquaintance she'd known from her days in the Army, Zachariah Jones. Though they'd butted heads while deployed at the same base in Afghanistan, they'd had enough in common to want to keep in touch.

Zach had just left the Army and come back to his home state of Montana. He'd taken a job with a man from Eagle Rock, Montana. A man who provided security services. What she needed now was someone who would have her back while she conducted her own investigation regarding what was happening on the reservation. She needed someone who could live with her on the reservation. Someone who was a member of the Blackfeet tribe.

Zach was her man.

CHAPTER 2

ZACHARIAH JONES HAD BEEN in Eagle Rock, Montana, for an entire week, familiarizing himself with the area, with his new position with the Brotherhood Protectors and with his boss, Hank Patterson, when he'd gotten the call from Lani Running Bear.

The woman had been, at first, a thorn in his side when he'd been at Bagram Air Base in Afghanistan. She'd been the MP who'd busted up the fight he'd gotten into with a Marine who'd tried to tell him that Army Rangers weren't nearly as effective as Navy SEALs.

Staff Sergeant Running Bear had taken him down and hauled his ass off to a temporary holding cell until his commanding officer came to collect him. Because his CO had been at a two-hour briefing, Zach had had enough time to get to know the hot MP who'd busted his ass.

17

Talk about a small world. He'd discovered she was from Montana, like him. And that she was Blackfeet, like him. Well, he was a watered-down version of Blackfeet, his grandmother having been one hundred percent Blackfeet. He'd been intrigued by her and impressed by her desire to return to Montana to help the people of her tribe.

When Zach had left Montana, he'd had no desire to return. However, after twelve years in the Army and too many deployments to count, he'd been ready to go home. He might not have been as eager to get back to Montana if he hadn't heard of the Brotherhood Protectors from one of his former teammates, Kujo, also known as Joseph Kuntz. He'd been with the Brotherhood for a couple years and spoke highly of his boss, former Navy SEAL Hank Patterson.

Having a job waiting for him after leaving the military had been a godsend. Too many of his compatriots who'd gotten out, thinking life was better as a civilian, had been gravely mistaken when they didn't find a place to fit in. The Brotherhood Protectors valued the skills they'd learned while fighting in the Middle East and other places around the world. They put those hard-earned skills to use protecting people who couldn't protect themselves.

But after a full week of getting used to being back in Montana, Zach was ready for an assignment, a purpose...some action.

When Lani's call had reached him, he'd been hesitant. He wanted to help her, but he had yet to prove himself to Hank and the Brotherhood.

He'd promised he'd help, but he had to clear it with his new boss first. Hank might have found an assignment for him, in which case, he'd have to assign one of the other men working for him to cover.

Zach drove out to Hank's place on the White Oak Ranch.

Sadie met him at the door, carrying their toddler, Emma, on her hip. "Zach, I'm glad you came. Hank's been talking about you."

Zach grimaced. "Has he found an assignment for me?"

She shook her head. "Not yet, but it won't be long. Seems the word has gotten out about the Brotherhood Protectors. Many of my fellow actors have asked for bodyguards. Once they have one of Hank's guys, they're hooked and spread the word. And, with so many people from California discovering the beauty of Montana, we have more and more opportunities to provide security here in the state."

"Zach," Hank's voice sounded from inside. "Come on in. Swede and I were working on something in the war room. Come on down."

"Yes, sir." Zach tipped his cowboy hat at Sadie and chucked Emma beneath her chin. "Good to see you, Mrs. Patterson."

"Oh, please, call me Sadie." She stepped aside to allow him to enter the house. "I'll bring coffee."

Zach shook hands with Hank and followed him into the basement headquarters of the Brotherhood Protectors.

"What brings you out?" Hank asked. "Not that you need a reason to come…"

"I had a call from an Army acquaintance I knew back at Bagram Air Base," Zach started without preamble. "She needs help and wanted to know if I could come to her assistance."

Hank's brow puckered. "What's her situation? I like to know the right person with the right skillset is assigned to a job."

"She's working a murder investigation and needs someone to watch her back," Zach said.

Hank nodded. "And why does she think you're the right man for the job?"

"She knows I'm a prior Army Ranger," Zach said.

"So are Taz and Viper," Hank pointed out.

Zach smiled. "Is either one of them Blackfeet?"

"Blackfeet?"

"Lani Running Bear is a member of the Blackfeet Nation. To live on the reservation, you have to be Blackfeet."

Hank raised a brow. "And you are?"

Zach lifted one shoulder. "My grandmother on my father's side was one hundred percent. I'm in the Blackfeet registry as a quarter Blackfeet."

Hank grinned. "I guess that makes you the right man for the job."

Zach frowned. "Look, I'm pretty sure this isn't a paying job."

"She needs help, right?"

Zach nodded. "Sure sounded like it."

"Then it's a legit job." His brow furrowed. "You'll be on your own out there, but we're only a call and plane ride away should you need backup."

"Anyone need some coffee?" Sadie descended the steps into the basement, carrying a tray of brimming coffee mugs.

Zach hurried over to take the tray from her. "I could use a cup."

"How are you going to arrive at the reservation?" Hank asked.

Setting the tray on the large conference table, Zach took one of the cups of coffee, frowning. "I could go, claiming my one quarter Blackfeet heritage."

"Won't you make them suspicious by showing up the day after a double murder?" Hank asked.

"You have a good point." Zach sipped the steaming cup of coffee. "Lani said they only allow Blackfeet to live on the reservation, and I'd need to be on the reservation to help keep her safe and find the killer."

"And how well do you know Lani?" Sadie asked, handing a cup of coffee to Swede.

"We met at Bagram Air Base in Afghanistan," Zach said. "We kept in touch because of our connection to the Blackfeet tribe."

"Is she married?" Sadie asked.

With a frown, Zach answered, "Not that I know of. She was single when we were deployed together."

"Then why don't you show up as her boyfriend." Sadie handed Hank a cup of coffee. "Or better yet, as her fiancé. That way, they would expect you to be with her and live in the same house."

"You think the tribal elders will buy that story?" Zach asked.

Sadie gave him a sassy smile. "Only if you make your engagement appear real."

"How do I do that?" Zach asked.

Sadie laughed. "You demonstrate your love, the reason the two of you are engaged," she said, her hand fisting on her hip.

Zach's brow twisted. "How do I do that?"

"Really, Zach?" Sadie shook her head. "You hold her hand in public. Kiss her sometimes, and put a ring on her finger. Do enough public displays of affection, and you'll have them fooled."

Zach frowned. "I don't know…"

"Do you have a better idea?" Hank asked, arching an eyebrow.

"No," Zach said, rubbing the back of his neck. He didn't know what Lani would think of that idea.

"I'll be right back." Sadie climbed the stairs and

Zach thanked the Pattersons, climbed into his truck and set off on the four-hour road trip to Browning, Montana, the headquarters of the Blackfeet Reservation.

As he passed through the small town of Eagle Rock, he tried to call Lani on his cellphone, but he didn't get an answer. Soon, he was out of town and in a dead zone of cellphone coverage. He'd have to fill her in when he reached her home. Hopefully, she'd go along with his cover.

His lips twitched. Seemed like a little turnabout was fair play—from Lani busting him in Afghanistan to needing his help in Montana. He liked being on the other end of this situation. Maybe he could prove to Hank, and to Lani, that he wasn't a screw-up. He had skills that would come in handy should anyone try to harm Lani.

LANI SLEPT FOR SIX HOURS, knowing she'd need the rest in order to be her sharpest when she went out on her own to question some of the people who were closest to the victims.

By the time she awoke, the sun was on its downward trajectory toward the ridges of the Rocky Mountains less than a hundred miles away. Anxious to find out what had happened in the murder investigation, she called Black Knife.

"Black Knife," her boss answered.

"Chief, Running Bear here. What have you heard on the Lightfoot and Wolf Paw murders?" She held her breath, not knowing what kind of answer she'd get from the chief of police. Especially since he'd told her she was off the case.

"The FBI has transferred the bodies to the Glacier County Coroner for examination. That's all we have so far. Not that it's any of your concern." His tone was tight, his words clipped.

She wrinkled her nose. "I promised Mattie Lightfoot I'd do my best to find out who killed her grandson," Lani said.

"You shouldn't have promised anything," the chief said.

"Well, I did, and I'm not going to let her down."

"You're off until further notice. Don't let me or any of the tribal elders find you're asking about the murders."

"Are you telling me to stay out of it?"

"I'm saying...don't let me or anyone else find out you're asking about the murders," Black Knife repeated, speaking slowly, as though to a dimwitted child.

"Yes, sir," she said and ended the call and stared at the phone.

That conversation was odd.

Had her boss given her roundabout permission to conduct her own investigation into the murders?

He hadn't said don't do it. He'd only said don't get caught.

She wondered what her boss really meant. However, whether he did or didn't want her snooping around, she was going to do it anyway. She'd made a promise to a friend, and Lani didn't break her promises.

She showered, blow-dried her hair and French braided it to get it out of her face. Since she wasn't working until further notice, she left her uniform hanging in the closet and pulled on a pair of jeans and a pale green, short-sleeved sweater that fit her to perfection. She was lacing up a pair of hiking boots when a knock sounded on the door to her cabin.

She rose from the chair she'd been sitting on, crossed to the entryway and pulled open the door.

Raymond Swiftwater stood in the doorway, flanked on either side by the Spotted Dog brothers.

"Ray," she said and dipped her head slightly. "What are you doing here?"

"The tribal elders are concerned you won't leave the murder investigations to the FBI and Police Chief Black Knife. I'm here to reiterate, you're not to work the case."

Lani crossed her arms over her chest. "I'm curious. Why are they so concerned about me?"

"The elders see you as a loose cannon. Ever since you returned from your stint in the Army, you've walked around like you own the place."

"I don't know what you're talking about. If you mean I'm a competent female law enforcement officer, then yes, I walk around with confidence. Does my self-assurance intimidate you or the other tribal elders?" She lifted her chin and met his gaze square on.

Swiftwater snorted. "Hardly. We think you're too full of yourself, and that you don't have any experience being a police officer on the rez."

"I was born and raised on this reservation. I spent ten years on active duty in the Army as a military police officer and survived six deployments." She squared her shoulders and met his gaze head-on. "I'd say I have the experience necessary to provide law enforcement to my people."

For a long moment, Swiftwater stared down his nose at her. "I only warn you to keep you from getting hurt."

Lani snorted. "Yeah. Well, thank you for your concern."

A truck pulled up beside Swiftwater's large SUV.

A man Lani barely recognized stepped out of the vehicle, his eyes narrowing at the men standing on Lani's porch.

It took Lani a full thirty seconds to place the man. As soon as he grinned, she knew. Her heart fluttered against her ribs, and heat climbed up her neck into her cheeks.

"If you're finished with your warning, I have

better things to do." She pulled the door closed behind her, stepped past Swiftwater and the Spotted Dog brothers and raced down the steps.

"Zach, I'm so glad you got here." She flung her arms around his neck and hugged him tight. "I didn't expect you for a few more days."

Zachariah Jones wrapped his arms around her waist and pulled her close. "I freed up sooner than I expected, and I thought I'd surprise you."

She pasted a smile on her face and leaned back in his arms. "I'm glad you did. It's been too long." He was going along with her ruse better than she'd expected. "Want to come inside?"

Zach set her at arm's length and shook his head. "Not until I say what I came here to say…"

Lani's brow dipped. "What is it, sweetheart?"

"I know it's kind of sudden, but I had a lot of time to think about it once I notified my CO I was leaving the military."

Lani wasn't sure what he was talking about, but she went along with it. "What have you been thinking about?"

"This." He stuck his hand in his pocket, pulled out a ring and dropped to one knee. "Lani Running Bear, you're the love of my life. Will you marry me?"

Lani stood in stunned silence. Of all things Zach could have said, *Will you marry me?* wasn't something Lani expected. "Uh…I don't know what to say."

He looked up at her and winked. "Just say yes."

She frowned. "Yes." The word came out more of a question than a commitment.

Zach stood, gathered her in his arms and kissed her soundly on the lips.

Lani didn't even try to stop him. She was too stunned to think.

Zach ended the kiss, pressed his lips to her ear and whispered, "Go along with it. It's my cover." He leaned back and grinned. "You don't know how happy you've just made me."

"Not as happy as I am," she said, falling into the ruse, even if her words were a little stiff.

Zach slipped the ring on her finger and smiled. "It fits."

"How did you know what size I wear?" she asked, staring down at the fat stone, twinkling up at her.

"I got it from your roommate in Afghanistan," he said.

"Tessa? You were thinking about this all along?" She shook her head and smiled up at him.

He chuckled. "Were you surprised?"

"I didn't think you even liked me," she said, thankful the statement was the truth.

"I didn't...at first." He lifted her hand and pressed a kiss to her ring finger. "No man likes it when a woman takes him down and hauls him off to confinement. But you grew on me, as I hoped I grew on you."

"Yes!" She flung her arms around his neck again,

putting on a show for Swiftwater. Later, she'd tell him how brilliant his cover story was. Right now, she had to convince the elder of its truth. When she settled back on her feet, she turned with a smile toward Raymond Swiftwater and the Spotted Dog brothers. "Elder Swiftwater, this is Zachariah Jones, my...fiancé." She hooked her hand through his arm and drew Zach toward Swiftwater.

Swiftwater's eyes narrowed. "You do realize you have to be Blackfeet to live on the reservation."

Lani grinned and hugged Zach's arm. "That was one of the reasons we hit it off so well when we were deployed. When I told him I was Blackfeet, he let me know his grandmother was one-hundred percent Blackfeet. It was such a cool coincidence to meet one of my people in such a faraway land."

His eyes narrowing even more, Swiftwater harrumphed. "I'll have to check into that." He lifted his chin. "Your grandmother's name?"

Zach raised an eyebrow in challenge. "Margaret Red Hawk. She's in the registry, as am I. My mother was sure to add me as soon as I was born."

Swiftwater snorted. "Only a quarter Blackfeet."

"But he satisfies the quantum test. A quarter meets the requirement, allowing Zach to live on the rez," Lani said. She let her hand slide down Zach's arm to his hand. Gripping it firmly, she smiled up at him like she thought a newly engaged woman should. "Come on, I'll show you our home."

Lani walked past Swiftwater, up the stairs and into the house.

Once inside, she started to let go of his hand.

Zach held tight and led her toward the front picture window. "He's still standing there. We need to give him one more reason to believe." He positioned them in front of the window and pulled her into his arms. "Make it count."

She leaned up on her toes and pressed her lips to his.

He snorted. "That wasn't very convincing."

She stared up into his eyes and cocked an eyebrow. "You can do better?"

Zach wrapped one arm around her middle and pressed her body to his. With his free hand, he cupped the back of her head and claimed her mouth in a kiss that left her knees weak and her heart pounding against her ribs so hard she was certain he could feel it against his chest. Not to mention the flood of heat coiling low in her belly. Holy hell.

When he finally let her breathe again, she didn't want his mouth to leave hers.

"That ought to do it," he said, and smiled down at her.

Stunned and a little dizzy, Lani leaned back against the arm around her waist and looked around him to the front yard where Swiftwater still stood, staring at the house.

She waved at the man and grinned broadly.

The elder turned, marched to his Denali and climbed into the back, while the Spotted Dog brothers took the front two seats.

Lani waited until they had driven out of sight before she stepped out of Zach's arms and smoothed her hair out of her face. That kiss had thrown her off balance, more than she'd like to admit. Especially to the man she'd hauled off to confinement during her deployment. Still… "You don't know how glad I am to see you."

"Just so you know, my boss made you my first assignment." He pulled her into his arms and hugged her like a long-lost friend. "But don't worry, I was coming anyway. How could I ignore a call from my favorite MP?" He winked. "I'm almost certain you saved me from an ass-whipping with that Marine."

"I doubt that. You were on top of him." She fought the urge to touch her throbbing lips with her fingertips. When he let go of her, she ran her gaze over him. "You've lost weight."

"My last deployment was tough on me. I got really tired of MREs."

"So, you quit eating?" Lani shook her head. "I guess the least I can do is feed you while you're here. But that'll have to be later." She glanced again out the window. "Now that Swiftwater is gone, I'd like to go talk to a few people. Are you ready to jump in with both feet?"

"I'm ready," he said. "You can fill me in on the way."

They exited the little house together.

When Lani started toward her SUV, Zach snagged her arm and turned her toward his vehicle. "Let's take mine. Not everyone knows it yet."

She nodded. "Good point," she said, and climbed up into the truck and fastened her seat belt.

Zach slid in behind the steering wheel and backed out of the driveway. "Where to?"

"Conrad," Lani said. On the way to Conrad, she filled him in on Tyler Lightfoot and Ben Wolf Paw's murders. "We're going to Conrad to talk to Tyler's girlfriend."

And in the meantime, Lani would try her darnedest to forget that kiss. It had all been for show.

On Zach's part, at least.

Lani had felt something she'd never felt before—a spark, a flame…hell…*an inferno*—when Zach had kissed her so thoroughly.

That's what she got for going so long without dating. She really needed to get out more often. And she would…after she caught the murderer.

CHAPTER 3

ZACH LISTENED to Lani's detailed description of the deaths of Lightfoot and Wolf Paw and cringed at the horror and pain they'd experienced. He chose to focus on the investigation, rather than the kiss that had started as part of his cover and ended as so much more.

Yeah, he'd been attracted to the black-haired, sexy MP when she'd taken him down and held him until his CO could claim him. He remembered her light, curvy body pressed against his as she'd nailed him to the ground in a pretty impressive move. Not only was she built the right way, she was strong and athletic, something he admired in a woman. He figured, if she was asking for help, she had bigger problems than wrestling with a couple of testosterone-heavy guys.

"What exactly do you want me to do?" he asked, when she'd finished outlining the situation.

"I'm going to be poking my head into an investigation where I've been told to butt out. I need you to watch my back. Someone has violently murdered two people already. When I start asking around about who could have done it, I don't want someone sneaking up on me. You're to be the eyes in the back of my head, as well as a second set of eyes on the evidence."

Zach nodded. "Okay, but I'm not an MP. I don't know how investigations go."

"No, but you're trained in combat. You might need that training if something goes wrong. And who else can I trust, if I can't trust an Army Ranger?" She gave him a lopsided grin.

"I've got your six," he said, feeling the weight of responsibility and accepting it. He was in an entirely different environment from his deployments in Iraq, Afghanistan, Syria and other places all over the world. Use of deadly force was something he had to keep to a minimum. Civilians didn't like it when people came through their hometowns guns ablazin'.

When they pulled up to the address she'd given him, Lani glanced over at him. "We need to keep up our cover. We're just here to express our condolences to Natalie, and I'll ask a few questions."

Zach nodded. "You're the cop. Take the lead."

She didn't wait for him to round the truck but got out and met him at the front fender.

Zach took her hand in his and gave her a hint of a smile as they walked toward the door of a white clapboard house with royal blue shutters.

Lani drew in a deep breath and knocked on the door.

A few moments later, the door opened, and an older man appeared, frowning.

"Mr. Preston?"

"Yeah." His eyes narrowed. "If you're here to talk to Natalie, she's not here."

"I'm sorry to hear that," Lani said. "We're friends of Tyler's family and only wanted to come to express our condolences. Could you please let her know Lani Running Bear, the officer who was first on scene, stopped by?"

Zach saw movement behind the man he assumed was Natalie's father. From the brief glimpse he caught, it appeared to be a young woman with blond hair. He squeezed Lani's hand.

She squeezed back and gave a nod to the man. "Thank you, Mr. Preston."

Zach turned with Lani and headed back to the truck. Once inside, he turned to Lani. "I saw someone behind Mr. Preston."

Lani nodded. "It was Natalie. Go slowly around the corner."

Zach shifted into drive and inched around the

corner. Even as slow as he was going, he had to slam on his brakes when a young woman ran out in front of him. It was the blonde he'd seen behind Mr. Preston.

Lani opened her door and started to get out. "Natalie?"

The woman ducked low and ran around to the passenger side of the truck. "Let me in," she said.

Zach popped the locks.

Natalie yanked open the back door and slid onto the seat, keeping her head down. "Go, go, go!" she urged.

"Before I do, are you eighteen?" Zach asked.

"Yes. I turned eighteen last month." Natalie sobbed. "Tyler took me out to my favorite restaurant for my birthday." Her words came out garbled as she fought and lost against the tears.

Zach pressed his foot to the accelerator and sped away from the Prestons' home.

When they'd gone a couple of blocks, he noticed a city park and pulled into an empty parking space.

As soon as Zach stopped the truck, Lani climbed out of the passenger seat and into the back with Natalie.

The young woman fell against her and buried her face in Lani's shirt.

Lani held her for a long time, stroking her hair and saying soothing words in the Blackfeet language.

When Natalie had spent her tears, she raised her head.

Zach handed her a napkin from his console.

She blew her nose and finally met Lani's eyes. "What happened? Why did Tyler die?"

"First of all, who told you he died?" Lani asked.

She drew in a shaky breath. "I had a visit from Police Chief Black Knife and an agent from the FBI. They said Tyler was...dead." She stopped, the tears flowing again.

Zach passed her another napkin.

Natalie wiped at the tears and blew her nose again. "I can't believe he's gone. I loved him so much. We were going to get married when he finished his schooling. We were going to move to Bozeman, away from the reservation, and have a lovely home and a couple of kids. All I had to do was wait." She stared at Zach. "Now, I have nothing."

"I'm so sorry," Lani said and continued to hold the woman in her arms, letting her cry until the sobs slowed to a stop.

"How...how did Tyler die?" Natalie asked.

Lani looked over her shoulder at Zach.

He held her gaze until Lani set Natalie at arms' length and looked her square in the eye. "Are you sure you want to know?"

Natalie nodded, tears trembling on her lashes.

Lani inhaled and let it out. "He was beaten and

stabbed multiple times. Then he was left inside his grandmother's trailer."

The young woman pressed her hands to her mouth, fresh streams of tears flowing down her face. "Why?" she wailed.

Lani shook her head. "I don't know. But I promised Mattie I would find the killer. I'll need your help."

Her brow wrinkled. "Isn't that what Police Chief Black Knife and the FBI are going to do? Do you work for the reservation law enforcement, too?"

"They pulled me off the case. I'm not supposed to be working right now." Lani squeezed Natalie's hands. "I made a promise to Mattie. I won't let her down. I won't let Tyler's death go unpunished."

"Who would do that to him?" Natalie whispered. "Tyler never hurt anyone."

"Natalie," Lani held the woman's hands in hers. "I need you to tell me everything you know down to the smallest detail that might have anything to do with you and Tyler."

"I told the chief and agent everything I knew." She shrugged. "What more could I say? What does it matter? It won't bring him back."

"Please, be patient if I repeat questions," Lani said. "Had Tyler had an argument with anyone recently?"

The young woman shook her head. "No. Everyone who knew him loved him. He was always so kind to everyone, even when they weren't kind to him."

"Were there people who were unkind to Tyler?" Lani asked.

Natalie's brow furrowed. "A couple months ago, some of the guys from my high school ganged up on him when we were at the Orpheum Theater. They didn't like the idea that he was from the reservation and dating a white girl." Natalie's lips thinned. "I told them to get lost and that I'd date Tyler before I dated any of them."

"Who were they? Can you give me their names?"

She nodded. "Russell Bledsoe, Dalton Miller and Brent Sullivan. But that was months ago. They haven't bothered us since I graduated from high school in June."

Lani pulled a pad and pen from her shirt pocket and jotted down the names. "You were with Tyler last night?"

Zach watched as Lani continued her questioning, calm and empathetic. If he were Natalie, he'd have spilled every detail to the capable and caring cop. She was as competent now as she'd been on the base at Bagram.

Natalie nodded. "He brought me home about ten o'clock." She dipped her head. "My father insists on a curfew, even though I'm old enough to make my own decisions. And since I still live with my parents, I have to live by their rules. Tyler walked me to the door and...everything."

"How did your father feel about Tyler? Did he have issue with him being Blackfeet?" Lani asked.

"At first. But, like I said, anyone who knew Tyler...really knew him, loved him. Even my father." She gave a crooked grin that turned downward with more tears. "My father helped him apply for college. He wanted any man who married his daughter to be able to support her."

"Did they have any harsh words or arguments that you know of?"

Natalie shook her head. "No."

"Did you visit the reservation often?" Lani asked. "Do you know who his friends are, where he likes to hang out?"

Natalie gave her a watery smile. "He took me to some of the events on the reservation. He was so very proud of his heritage. We went horseback riding with some of his friends and had picnics. Tyler was always careful to take good care of me. He wanted me to be happy."

Lani sat silently, waiting for Natalie to give her details.

Zach admired her unflappability. He doubted he could be so patient.

Natalie closed her eyes. "His best friend is Jonathon Spotted Eagle. His other friends are Ashley Morning Star and Jesse Davis."

"Where were his favorite places to hang out?" Lani asked, her voice low, persistent, but gentle.

"He liked to go to Jonathon's place. Jonathon's mother works late at a bar in Browning. He'd go there after dropping me off. He and Jonathon either watched television or played video games late into the night. He'd text me when he'd head home to his grandmother's place."

"Tyler was attending college, wasn't he?" Lani asked.

"Yes, ma'am. He was going to the community college in Browning. He was awarded a scholarship to attend based on his grades in high school. He was going to do two years close to home, and then transfer to Montana State in Missoula to finish out his degree. He had everything going for him. He was studying to be an engineer. I was going to start at Montana State this fall. He was going to join me in a year." Her voice caught on a sob. "He was so smart and had everything going for him." She buried her face in her hands and cried.

Lani gave her a moment before she asked, "Was Tyler out of school for the summer?"

Natalie scrubbed the tears from her face and sat up. "Yes. He worked during the summer to have money for the fall and spring semesters, so that he could concentrate on his studies."

"Where did he work?" Lani asked.

"At a ranch near Cut Bank...the K Bar L

43

Ranch. It's a pretty large ranch, over a hundred thousand acres. The owner is also the owner of some sports teams." Natalie's brow dipped. "The ranch foreman he worked for is Patrick Clemons."

"Did he do any other odd jobs in or around Browning?" Lani asked.

"On weekends, he helped clean Mick's Bar," Natalie said. "He was supposed to work there this morning. When he didn't text me, as usual, I called Mick's to see if he'd left his phone at home. He never made it there."

Zach glanced at the clock on his dash. They'd been sitting there for over twenty minutes. "Natalie, will your father be worried about you?"

Natalie looked up. "How long have I been with you?"

"About twenty minutes," Zach said.

"Oh, dear." She started to get out of the truck. "I need to go home. Daddy will be beside himself."

Lani laid a hand on her arm. "We'll get you close faster than you can walk."

The younger woman nodded.

Zach pulled out of the parking lot and turned back the direction they'd come.

Lani's voice continued in the back seat. "Natalie, if you can think of anything else. Anyone Tyler might have had contact with last night, an argument he might have had, anything, call me."

In the rearview mirror, Zach saw her hand Natalie a business card.

"The number on the back is my cellphone number. I don't care what time of day or night you call," Lani added.

Natalie clutched the card in her hand. "Thank you for caring about Tyler. I hope you find who did this."

By then, Zach was one block away from the white clapboard house with the blue shutters.

"Stop here," Natalie said.

Zach pulled to the curb and waited as Natalie climbed down from the truck.

"Be careful," Lani said. "We don't know who did this, or who he'll go after next."

"Don't worry. My father won't let me out of his sight for long." Natalie hurried back to her house and entered through the back door.

Zach waited until she was inside, and the door was closed.

Lani slipped out of the back seat and climbed up into the passenger seat.

"Where to?" Zach asked. "Want to interview the boys from the theater?"

Lani shook her head. "Not yet." She hit some keys on her cellphone. "Christina, Lani Running Bear here. I need a favor. I need Ben Wolf Paw's next of kin's address. Then I need you to look up addresses for the following people in Conrad, Montana—Russell Bledsoe, Dalton Miller and Brent

Sullivan. Yeah, I'm not supposed to be involved in the investigation, but I'm off for a couple of days and need something to keep me occupied. If you could keep this between you and me, I'd appreciate it."

Zach listened as Lani did what she did best.

He was impressed and inspired by her dedication and determination to find who had killed Tyler and Ben. What she was doing was gathering the pieces of a puzzle. Zach was already caught up in the investigation and was just as eager now to get to the bottom of the murders.

ONCE LANI HAD the address for Ben Wolf Paw's next of kin, she gave Zach the information and sat back, thinking through everything Natalie had said.

"What I'm not seeing yet is the connection between Tyler Lightfoot and Ben Wolf Paw. They didn't run in the same circles. Ben was at least fifteen years older than Tyler. But whoever killed Tyler also killed Ben. The murders were too similar to be a coincidence. And they were dumped, rather than being left where they were murdered."

"Did they find the victims' vehicles?" Zach asked.

"I don't know." She dialed Christina again, kicking herself for not thinking about the victims' vehicles.

Her friend answered on the first ring. "Lani, you're going to get me into trouble," she whispered.

"Are Police Chief Black Knife and the FBI agent in the office right now?" Lani asked.

"Yes," Christine said, her voice cryptic.

"Can you tell me if they found the victims' vehicles?" Lani asked.

"Yes."

"Thanks. That's all I need for now." Lani ended the call.

"You didn't ask where they found them," Zach said.

"She couldn't talk. The police chief and FBI agent were in the office. Besides, I know who to ask." Lani pointed to the next road ahead. Before we leave Cut Bank, we'll go there first, then to Ben's family."

Zach followed her directions to the Glacier County impound lot where the vehicles had been delivered.

When they arrived, Lani climbed down out of Zach's truck and headed for the office at the center of the lot.

Zach followed, giving her a feeling of reassurance. Not that she felt any sense of danger at the impound lot. It was nice that she didn't have to ask him to follow her. He did it on his own.

"Pete?" she called out as she neared the office door.

An older, grizzled man emerged from the building. "Officer Running Bear, what brings you to my lot?"

"Good to see you, Pete. How's your wife?" Lani held out her hand.

Pete took it and gave it a firm shake. "She's getting over a cold. Otherwise, we're doing okay. The kids are coming up from Bozeman this weekend."

"I know that will make Betty happy to see them." Lani dropped his hand and turned to Zach. "This is my fiancé, Zach Jones."

Pete shook Zach's hand. "Congratulations."

Zach nodded. "Thanks."

Lani asked, "Did you get a couple of vehicles in from the rez today?"

Pete frowned. "I did." He nodded toward a corner of the lot where an older model, blue Ford truck sat. Lani recognized the vehicle as Tyler's. Beside it was a black SUV.

"Mind if we take a look?" Lani asked.

Pete shrugged and started toward the vehicles. "Your boss and an FBI agent were here an hour ago to look them over. I wouldn't actually touch them until they've had a chance to dust for prints and whatever else they do."

"We won't touch. We just want to look." Lani followed Pete. "Who brought them in?"

"Whitegrass Towing. Dan and Isaac brought them in a few hours ago." Pete shook his head. "Sad to hear about the two murders on the reservation. I don't suppose you know who did it…?"

Lani shook her head. "Not yet. We're working on it."

Pete frowned. "Why aren't you working with the Chief of Police and the FBI agent?"

"I'm not officially on the case," Lani said. She touched Pete's arm. "I'd appreciate it if you didn't mention my visit to anyone."

Pete's eyes narrowed. "You asking me to lie?"

Lani shook her head. "No. But if no one asks…"

The old man's lips twitched. "Gotcha."

Her jaw tightening, Lani said, "I promised Mattie Lightfoot I'd find her grandson's killer."

"I'm glad there are good cops out there," Pete said. "The media gives them a bad name. Thank you for being one of the good guys."

Lani circled Tyler's old truck, careful not to touch it. The crime scene experts would dust for fingerprints and search for any other evidence they might find.

From all outward appearances, Tyler's vehicle appeared normal. Lani couldn't see any blood on the outside or inside through the windows. As violent as the murders had been, if the victim had been in or near his vehicle, there would have been some blood spatter. Unless the murderer cleaned the vehicle after performing his heinous crime.

After she'd looked over Tyler's truck, she moved to Ben's SUV. An older model vehicle. It had more trash inside it, including old food wrappers, empty soda cans and junk mail. Again, just by looking through the window, Lani couldn't see any blood or signs of struggle. The trash appeared to be scattered, but not like it would have been had the driver been attacked inside the SUV.

"See anything that helps?" Pete asked.

Lani shook her head. "No."

Pete nodded. "That's pretty much what the chief and FBI agent said."

"Thanks for letting me take a look." Lani held out her hand to the older man. "Say hello to your wife. I hope she feels better."

"Will do," Pete said. "And you be careful out on the reservation. Hate to think there's a killer loose."

Lani followed Zach to his truck and climbed in, unease tugging at her belly. She waited until he'd pulled onto the highway until she spoke. "Did you notice anything about those two vehicles?"

Zach shrugged. "I didn't see anything out of the ordinary. Did you see anything I missed?"

Lani shook her head. "No. That's just it. If they were driving when they came across the murderer, they stopped the vehicle and got out before the confrontation occurred."

"It would help to know where their vehicles were found," Zach said.

"Right. If they were found on a deserted road versus at a convenience store, it will tell us a little more about the murderer."

"Like?" Zach prompted.

"If they were found on a deserted road, the victims could have stopped to help someone supposedly stranded. It's quite possible they knew the person who murdered them, especially if the vehicles were found on the rez."

"What do the two victims have in common? Why were they targeted?"

Lani frowned. "Other than they are both from the reservation, I don't know. They don't have the same friends or work at the same location."

"There has to be a connection."

"Agreed. But so far, I don't have one in mind," Lani said.

Zach pulled out onto the road. "Where to next?"

"Whitegrass Towing. We need to know where those vehicles were found." She gave him the directions to the towing company located in Browning.

To fill the silence and because she was curious, Lani, asked, "So, what's your story? Why did you get out of the military? I would have thought you'd stay until you at least hit twenty." She looked across the console at him. "Were you medically retired? Or had you had enough?"

Zach gave her crooked smile. "I'd had enough deployments. I guess when you busted me in Bagram, you reminded me of home." He snorted softly. "Up to that point, I'd never thought I'd come back to Montana."

Her lips twitched on the corners. She'd felt much the same. Joining the military had gotten her out of Montana. Once out, all she could think about was going back and helping fix some of the things that were broken on the rez. Too many of her people were on a slow path to nowhere. The military had shown her that she had choices in life. Every person was the master of his or her own destiny. She didn't have to wait for life to happen. She could make the changes necessary to be healthy and happy. It was all about attitude and the right choices. Lani hoped she could instill some of her positivity into the local youth and help them find a path that led them to success.

As part of her determination to help, she'd signed on with the Blackfeet Law Enforcement Services and volunteered at the local high school to help the teenagers with career planning. In some cases, she'd been helping them study for college placement exams and applying for universities. Her parents hadn't known how to help her along those lines, never having been to college themselves. Lani's platoon sergeant had used his down-time to take online college courses. He'd encouraged all the members of his platoon to do the same. He'd taken Lani under his wing and helped her fill out the necessary forms to enroll and request her high school transcripts.

He'd helped get her started taking college courses while she was on active duty. Using the GI bill, she planned on finishing her undergraduate degree. Then she'd either teach or join the Montana State Police. She had options. The reservation children needed to know they had options as well.

"What about you?" Zach asked. "Why did you come back?"

Lani shrugged and stared out the window. "I missed Montana. Don't get me wrong. The Army was good for me. It got me off the reservation and taught me there was more to life than the rampant unemployment you find on the rez."

Zach's brow twisted. "And you came back anyway?"

She gave him a crooked grin. "Yeah. I wanted to do what I could to help others who might be feeling hopeless."

Zach chuckled. "Another do-gooder?"

Lani frowned. "Another?"

"Your victim, Tyler. From what you said about him, he was good to others." Zach's smile faded.

Lani frowned. "Tyler was a good young man. Always doing things for his grandmother and anyone else who needed help." Was that the connection? Was the murderer targeting nice people? Lani shook her head. At that moment, they arrived at the outskirts of Browning.

"Turn at the first street to your right," Lani directed. She hoped the location where the vehicles were found would give her a clue.

CHAPTER 4

Zach turned at the first street in Browning and parked in front of a building with a tow truck out front. The lettering on the tow truck read Whitegrass Towing.

Lani hopped down out of Zach's truck.

He joined her in front. Together, they walked into the building.

Inside, the air smelled of old oil, grease, rubber and cigarettes.

A dark-haired man sat in a dilapidated swivel chair, his booted feet propped on the counter in front of him. He blew a stream of smoke into the air and stared over the tops of his boots at Zach then Lani. "Running Bear, who's your friend?"

Lani tipped her head toward Zach and gave the man an easy smile. "Isaac Whitegrass, this is Zach Jones...my...fiancé." She slipped her arm through

Zach's and turned her smile up at him. "I just got engaged."

Isaac's feet slipped off the counter and dropped with bang on the floor. He pushed to his feet and held out his hand. "Nice to meet you." He nodded toward Lani. "You got a good one there. Her heart's in the right place. Not sure I would ever cross her though. I hear she can throw down a man twice her size in the blink of an eye."

Zach nodded. "I've been the recipient of just such a throw." He chuckled. "I completely underestimated her."

Isaac grinned. "I bet that was a mistake."

"Not at all. You could say that she swept me off my feet. I fell in love at first body slam." He slipped his arm around Lani and pulled her close. "Isn't that right?"

Lani pinned a smile on her face that was as fake as a wooden nickel. "Yes, that's right."

Isaac glanced from Lani to Zach and back to Lani. "You here about the two vehicles we towed to Cut Bank earlier today?"

Lani nodded. "We are. Would you mind telling us where you found them?"

Isaac scratched his dark head. "Got the same question from your boss and the FBI agent earlier."

Lani's smile relaxed. "I figured as much. I also figured it doesn't hurt to have more than a couple sets of eyes on a case in case someone misses something important."

"True." Isaac nodded. "I was sick over Tyler and Ben's deaths. They were some of the good guys."

Lani's lips twisted. "I promised Tyler's grandmother that I'd do my best to find his killer."

Isaac studied her for a long moment, before opening his mouth again. "Rusty Fenton called in an abandoned vehicle at the turn-off to Kipps Lake. Dan and I had been listening to the police scanner at the moment when Tyler's grandmother called in about Tyler. When Rusty notified us of the abandoned vehicle, we thought nothing of it...until we realized it was Tyler's old truck."

Another man, who looked remarkably like Isaac appeared in the doorway at the back of the shop, rubbing his greasy hands on a shop rag. "Who wants to know about Tyler's truck?" Dan Whitegrass asked. He frowned at Zach. Then his gaze went to Lani, and his frown deepened. "Who've you got with you?"

"Lani's got herself a man," Isaac said with a grin.

"He ain't Blackfeet," Dan said, his tone low.

"Actually, he's a quarter," Lani said.

Isaac and Dan both turned to Zach, eyebrows raised.

Zach squared his shoulders and lifted his chin, meeting their challenge. "My grandmother was one hundred percent," Zach said. "You can look her up. Margaret Red Hawk."

"I will," Dan said, but his frown lessened. "This is the second round of law enforcement personnel sniffing around, asking about Tyler and Ben's vehicles. You and the chief aren't working together on this case?"

Lani glanced away. "I wasn't assigned to it, but I promised Tyler's grandmother I'd make sure I found his killer."

Dan and Isaac nodded as one.

"I didn't like the FBI guy, anyway," Dan said. "Not Blackfeet."

"Yeah, but you know it's standard procedure for the FBI to help with murder investigations," Lani said. "I just want to be a second pair of eyes and fulfill my promise to Mattie."

"What do you need to know?" Dan asked.

"Where you found the two vehicles," Lani said.

Isaac answered. "I picked up Tyler's out by the turn-off to Kipps Lake."

"And I collected Ben's after the FBI agent and the police chief called us to a street a couple blocks away from the elementary school."

"Thanks," Lani said. "That's all I needed to know for now."

Zach slipped an arm around Lani's waist. "Ready to go?"

She leaned into him and smiled up into his eyes. "I am."

He liked the way she felt against him.

She turned her smile toward Isaac and Dan. "Thank you."

"We hope you find who did it. Tyler and Ben were good people," Dan said.

"And we have more faith in you than in the FBI," Isaac said. "They have yet to find Angel."

Zach turned her toward the door and walked with her out into the sunshine. "Who is Angel?"

"A missing teenaged girl. The last time she was seen or heard from was four months ago. She was on her cellphone talking to her boyfriend when she was cut off. No one has seen her since. The FBI were called in via the Bureau of Indian Affairs, but they weren't able to locate the girl. There are far too many missing or exploited women from the reservation."

"You think these cases are related?"

"No. Angel's body was never found. This murderer *wanted* Tyler and Ben to be found." Lani shook her head. "It doesn't make sense. Especially Tyler's murder. Why would he have been out by the lake so late at night? And there was no blood or sign of struggle inside or outside his vehicle."

"Unless he picked up his murderer and drove out to the lake with him in the vehicle," Zach suggested. "Then, when they reached the remote location, his attacker got him out of the vehicle before he stabbed him."

"In that case, Tyler had to have known the man," Lani said.

"And it had to be a man," Zach said, "to lift, drag or carry another full-grown man and shove him into a truck or the back seat of a vehicle to deposit him elsewhere."

"And he had to have staged his car at the lake." Lani's eyes narrowed. "We need to find the vehicle he used to stash the bodies as he moved them from the murder location to their final resting places."

Zach's eyes narrowed. "How many people live on the reservation?"

"A little over ten thousand."

His brow puckering, Zach shook his head. "That's a lot of vehicles to investigate."

"It all goes back to what Ben and Tyler had in common." Lani stared out the window. "Or were they just in the wrong place at the wrong time? Damn, it can't be that random."

Zach stopped before pulling out onto the road. "Where to?"

"We need to talk to Ben's brother." She gave him directions to Ben's house. "Ben lived with his older brother, Mark. Mark wasn't the best role model. He's been in and out of jail for possession of drugs and public intoxication. Ben bailed him out whenever he had the money to help. Mark was his only family."

"Where are their parents?"

"Long since passed," Lani said.

As he drove through Browning, Zach shot a glance toward Lani. "You like police work?"

She nodded. "I don't do it to be a pain, like a lot of people think about law enforcement personnel." Her lips twisted into a grimace. "I do it because I hope I can make a difference."

Zach chuckled. "Like saving two dumbasses from breaking each other's bones?"

She frowned. "Yeah. I didn't haul you in because I was on a power kick." Her lips quirked upward on the corners. "Although, I did get a kick out of taking you down."

"I let you."

She snorted. "Believe what you want. As far as your buddies are concerned, a woman got the better of you."

Zach lifted one shoulder and let it fall. "Yeah, I have to admit, my ego was bruised that day, along with my backside. My teammates gave me hell later, after the CO chewed me out." But he'd admired her strength and ability. He'd found it extremely sexy, not that he'd tell her and suffer another takedown.

He looked her way again.

Hell, he might just tell her and enjoy the takedown.

She turned, her eyes narrowing. "What are you smiling about?"

Zach quickly refocused on the road ahead. "Nothing. I just didn't realize how much I missed your intensity." Out of the corner of his eye, he could see her studying him, her brow puckering.

Then she glanced forward. "Turn here."

"Here?" he asked.

"Yes, here," she said.

With only seconds to respond, he stomped on the brakes and turned the steering wheel in time to leave the pavement and pull onto a rutted dirt road, leading up to a ramshackle mobile home with old tires on the roof, holding down a tattered tarp. A junk car stood in the drive with the hood up, the wheels removed and the chassis resting on concrete blocks. An old washer lay on its side to the right of the house and the steps leading up to the front door were faded wood, possibly rotten.

The truck was still rolling when Lani cursed, yanked open the door and leaped to the ground.

"What the hell?" Zach yanked the truck into park. Before he could get out of the vehicle, Lani had disappeared around the back of the trailer.

As they'd driven up to the trailer, Lani spied Mark Wolf Paw staring out the window of the trailer. His eyes widened, and he twisted the blinds closed. He was going to run.

Lani didn't wait for the truck to come to a full stop. She shoved the door open and jumped down, hitting the ground running.

If Mark got away, they wouldn't be able to question him about his brother. Mark was known to get lost for weeks at a time, if he thought he might be in trouble.

Lani really needed to talk to him. He could be the key to identifying the killer. She couldn't let the bastard run. He owed it to his little brother to stick around and answer a few questions.

As she ran around the side of the trailer, the back door slammed open.

The man who jumped to the ground raced away without looking back.

Lani gave chase, running as fast as she could.

Before she could get close enough, he hopped onto an old dirt bike, revved the engine and spun in the dirt before the threadbare tires engaged and shot the motorcycle forward.

Lani didn't slow; she kicked up her pace and ran after him.

She flung herself at the man, her hand catching on his jacket.

Mark jerked backward but kept his grip on the handlebar. The bike spun to the side. Mark regained his balance, shrugged off her grip and goosed the throttle, sending it speeding away.

Still running when Mark forced her to let go, Lani stumbled and fell forward. Tucking her body, she hit the ground, rolled to her side and was on her feet again within the next second. But it was too late.

Mark was a plume of dust rising up from the dry prairie.

As she stood watching the man disappear in a cloud of dry soil, hands descended on her shoulders.

Zach spun her toward him. "Are you all right?" he asked, his breathing coming in short gasps.

Dragging in a steadying breath, Lani nodded. "I am. But he got away, dammit."

"Please," Zach said, his fingers tightening on her upper arms. "Don't do that again. At least, warn me before you jump out of a moving vehicle."

She gave him a sheepish grin. "Sorry. I saw him looking at us in the window. I knew he'd make a run for it." Lani tipped her head toward the settling prairie dust. "And he did. I'd hoped I could catch him before he got away."

"You asked me to watch your back." He pulled her into his arms and rested his chin on top of her head. "How can I do that if you're running off without me?"

"I'm sorry." She leaned her cheek against his chest and listened to the wild beating of his heart. Had she scared him? Or was it just exertion from trying to catch up to her? Whatever it was, she liked the way his arms felt around her. She liked it too much. Lani inhaled the scent of Zach. He smelled the same as when she'd tackled him in Afghanistan. All male and sexy as hell. She'd spent more time with him when he'd been cooling his heels in the camp holding cell than she'd spent with any other soldier she'd yanked out of a fight. Though she hadn't admitted it to herself, she'd been intrigued with him, with his scent, with his heritage. And she'd been disappointed when his commanding officer had finally come to claim him. Yeah, she'd seen him around the camp, and had even spoken to him several times, but it hadn't been as intimate as when she'd thrown him to the ground and held him down with her body.

Having him hold her now was an entirely new experience and one she didn't really want to end.

What was she thinking? He was there to cover her six, not to tempt her into his bed. Not that he'd asked. But if he did...

Lani blinked, stiffened and forced herself to place her palms on the hard planes of his chest. At that point, she should have pushed him away. But she didn't. Instead, she let her hands absorb the warmth of him through his black T-shirt.

"Are you okay?" Zach asked. "You took a tumble chasing after Ben's brother."

She shook her head, feeling a little dizzy, but not from her fall. Lani raised her head and stared up into Zach's eyes.

Warning bells went off in her head.

"I was worried about you," Zach said. "He could have dragged you across the ground or run over you." Zach smoothed his thumb across her cheek and tucked a strand of her hair behind her ear. "See? You must have hit your head when you went down." He brushed his thumb against her right temple. "You have a small scrape there."

She shook her head, mesmerized by the concern pulling his brow low on his forehead. "I don't feel it," she murmured.

He smiled down at her. "I'm not surprised. You're bound to be hopped up on adrenaline." Then he did something amazing. He leaned forward and pressed his lips to her forehead. "Promise me you won't go all badass cop on me and run off on your own. He might have been carrying a weapon. You could have been shot."

"I'm a cop. I go after the bad guys."

"Yeah, but you have backup. Use me." Again, he pressed a soft kiss to her forehead. "Please."

"Don't," she said, shaking her head.

"Don't what?" he asked.

"Don't do that."

"Do what?"

Her cheeks heated. "Nothing." Finally, she found the strength and mental capacity to pull out of his arms and stand on her own. Maybe he was right. Maybe she'd hit the ground too hard and scrambled her brains.

Zach glanced at her once more before tipping his head toward the back door of the trailer that stood wide open. "Should we look inside to see if there's anything incriminating?"

Lani squared her shoulders and nodded. "Yes, we should."

"Do you have to have a warrant or anything?" he asked.

"The door was open. I assume he left it that way for me to go in." She turned away from Zach and strode toward the trailer. The backside was no better than the front side, with an array of old tires, car parts and trash lying in the dirt. The back steps were rickety wood, split and weather-worn. Lani mounted each step with caution, placing one foot at a time, testing each riser before entrusting her weight to the damaged wood. At the top, she ducked her head through the door into the dark interior, her nose wrinkling.

The window blinds had been drawn. Some of the windows had no blinds at all but were covered in a variety of old sheets or worn blankets. On a table against a wall were several plastic bags of white powder, syringes and other drug paraphernalia.

"He didn't appear to be too concerned about the death of his brother," Zach observed, his voice coming from over Lani's shoulder.

Lani's jaw firmed. "Mark wasn't concerned about anything but his next fix. Ben took care of him on more than one occasion when he was stoned out of his mind. Ben begged Mark to give it up. He even had him committed to a rehab facility against Mark's wishes. He only wanted his brother to be healthy and live to see his fortieth birthday. Why does it seem only the good die young?" She shook her head. "I'm going to leave the investigation to the chief. He needs to know what's going on here."

"I'd say." Zach frowned. "Do you think he might have killed his own brother?"

Lani shrugged. "It's possible. Ben put him into rehab before. He might have threatened to put him in rehab again." She tipped her chin toward the drugs. "Especially based on what's on that table. But what reason would he have had to kill Tyler?"

"Could the two murders be unrelated?" Zach asked.

"They could," Lani said, "but consider this: they occurred on the same night, each one was killed in a similar manner and in a location other than where his body was found. This leads me to believe they were killed by the same person or persons."

Zach nodded. "Make sense."

Lani pulled out her cellphone and glanced down at the screen. "No service out this far." She eased down the stairs and rounded the trailer.

Zach followed. "I can stay here while you take my truck back to town for potential cellphone reception."

She glanced back at the trailer. "I don't want to leave the place unprotected. Mark might return and clear the evidence. The other option is for you to go back to town, and I'll stay here." Her eyes narrowed.

"I actually think that's the better option. That way you're making the call. Not me. Since I'm off the case."

Zach's gut clenched. "I don't like leaving you here. What if Mark comes back?"

"I can handle him." Lani patted her jacket, beneath which she had her gun. "And I have my own protection, if he gets stupid."

"Why didn't you use it when he took off?" Zach asked.

"I wanted to question him." Her lips quirked. "Kinda hard to get answers out of a corpse."

Zach would rather she'd shot the bastard than get torn up being dragged behind the druggie on his motorcycle. "Still, how can I protect you, if you're here and I'm halfway back to town?"

"I'll take my chances." She motioned with her head. "There's not much a person can hide behind out here. I can see anything coming. If I feel threatened, I'll shoot first, ask questions later." She winked. "Please. Go. Call 911 and ask the dispatcher to send the chief."

Not happy about leaving her, Zach climbed into his truck and drove down the rutted path as fast as he could without tearing up his truck. Once on the paved road, he hit the accelerator and pressed it to the floor, watching his cellphone and the reception indicator on the screen. He was almost all the way to Browning before a single bar showed. Immediately, he slowed and dialed 911, passing on the information just as Lani had asked.

"Your name?" the dispatcher asked. Her voice sounded female.

"Zach Jones."

"Are you Lani's fiancé?" the dispatcher asked.

Hesitating for a second, he responded. "Yes."

"Congratulations. I hear you're a hunk."

He didn't know what to say to that. "You'll pass the word on to the chief?"

"I will. Keep my girl safe, will ya? She's the best thing to happen to the rez in a while."

Zach relaxed. Apparently, Lani had allies on the police force, even if she'd been pulled off the murder case. "I'll do my best."

Before he ended the call, he was turning his truck around, bumping onto the shoulder and down into a ditch before he regained the pavement. As quickly as he'd come, he was on his way back to Lani, his heart in his throat, his hands gripping the steering wheel so tightly his knuckles turned white. With as much product as had been left on the table, Zach wouldn't be surprised if Mark returned, ready to claim it. Even if he had to go through Lani to get to it.

CHAPTER 5

Lani circled the trailer several times while waiting for the chief or Zach to return. She didn't want to disturb the interior in case there was any evidence pertaining to the murders inside. At the very least, Mark could be brought in on possession charges, at which time, they could question him on his whereabouts at the times of the murders. The man could have killed his brother in a drug-induced rage, but her gut wasn't ready to believe it.

The two murders had to have been committed by the same person. They were too much alike. Lani couldn't come up with a single reason why Mark would have killed Tyler. They weren't related like Mark and Ben, and they didn't run in the same social circles. It didn't make sense.

And, based on the other vehicles outside the trailer, the only one operational had been the one

Mark had escaped on. A man couldn't load and carry a corpse on a motorcycle. Not far, anyway. Like Tyler's vehicle, Ben's hadn't seemed disturbed, as if he'd been killed in it, and then carried to an alternate location to be dumped.

She needed to see the coroner's report on the two victims. Had they fought back? Were there any signs they'd struggled, scratched or bruised their opponent before being beaten to death? If they had gotten in a punch, the murderer would have some marks. The sooner they found him, the better. Bruises and scratches faded after too much time.

With her attention on the plains around her, she heard the engine before she saw Zach's truck pull onto the rutted path leading up to the isolated trailer. She hated to admit it, but she was glad to see him. Had Mark returned, he might have been hopped up on whatever drug he'd left on the table. He could have come after her full of aggression and desperate to get his next fix. A bullet wouldn't necessarily stop him in his tracks.

Zach pulled into the littered yard and slid to a stop in the loose dirt.

Lani approached his truck as Zach dropped down.

He met her at the front fender and pulled her into his arms. "He didn't come back?"

She chuckled and rested her hands on his chest. "No. I didn't even have to take out my gun."

"Thank God," Zach said. "I was worried."

"I think you were gone all of five minutes. Not much can happen in that short time," she said. But she didn't pull out of his embrace. She liked how solid he felt against her.

The sound of another engine caught her attention.

Zach must have heard it too. His body stiffened, and he turned toward the rutted path he'd just come in on.

Her hand on her pistol, Lani watched. Not until she saw the lights on top of the vehicle did she relax slightly.

The chief's Blackfeet Law Enforcement vehicle came to a stop beside Zach's truck. Police Chief Black Knife climbed out of the front seat, frowning. "I thought I told you that you were off the case," he said without preamble.

Lani stepped away from Zach's arms. "I heard you," she said. "I was just checking on Mark to see how he was after hearing of his brother's death."

"And?"

Lani waved her hand toward the trailer. "See for yourself. He took off before I could ask."

Black Knife's frown deepened. "If he took off, what's there to see?"

"He left the back door wide open." Lani raised an eyebrow. "What he left inside is in plain sight."

The police chief rounded the trailer and climbed

the rickety back steps.

Lani followed and waited at the bottom of the steps. "Neither of us went inside. We didn't want to destroy any evidence."

"Good thing," the chief said. "I can get him on possession."

"Do you think he could have killed Ben?" Lani held up her hands. "Not that I'm investigating or anything. Just a concerned citizen with a valid question."

The chief shot a glance her way before disappearing inside the mobile home. A few moments later, he came to the door, shaking his head. "I didn't see anything he could have used to inflict the blunt force trauma both Tyler and Ben endured. But I have a reason to haul his ass in and question him."

"If you can catch him," Lani said. "He took off on a dirt bike. Knowing he'll be busted on possession, he might not come back."

"I'll put out a BOLO on him." He nodded toward Lani. "I have a stash of evidence bags and a camera in my vehicle."

"I'll get it." Lani turned and hurried around the trailer to the chief's service vehicle. In the glove compartment, she found the bags and the camera. When she returned to the back door of the trailer, Black Knife was inside opening cabinet doors.

Lani stepped past Zach, brushing against him on the steps. Her heart fluttered against her ribs, sending blasts of electricity through her senses. She hurriedly entered the trailer, carrying the items her boss had requested.

He held out his hand. "You shoot while I collect," he said.

Lani nodded and handed him the bags. As she snapped photos, Black Knife collected the drugs and paraphernalia. The table wasn't the only place with contraband. Several cabinets contained more blocks of white powder and bags full of pills.

Bedrooms at either end of the trailer were as different as night and day. One had a neatly made bed with carefully hung clothing in a small closet. Shoes were lined up on the floor and towels were folded on a shelf. At the opposite end of the trailer was what appeared to be a pile of filthy blankets shoved up against the wall. Lani wasn't sure the mattress had ever had a protective sheet on it. Empty beer cans lay amongst the blanket folds, along with an old pizza box, with a half-eaten pizza in it. The filthy room smelled as if someone had urinated in it and hadn't cleaned it up.

Lani pinched her nostrils. The scent was overwhelming. "Are you about done?" she asked.

"Almost." He lifted the mattress and looked beneath the bed. A large compartment contained even more of the white powder bricks. "There's no way this was for personal use. The bastard was selling." He held up the mattress while Lani clicked away.

Then he propped up the mattress and bagged the remaining drugs. "There's going to be a lot of unhappy people when they don't get their stuff."

"You need to send it on up to the state headquarters. If you keep that much product in the office, someone is liable to shoot up the place trying to get to it."

"Good point." He handed her several bags. "Let's get this into the trunk of my vehicle."

Lani helped carry the bags of evidence out to the chief's service vehicle and settle them into the trunk.

When all had been collected and stored in his trunk, the chief closed it and stared at Lani. "I know you're conducting your own investigation," he said.

Her gut clenching, Lani could only nod. She wouldn't lie to the man who'd taken a chance on hiring her. A man whom she looked up to and admired.

"Don't...stop," he said. "Don't stop. We need all eyes on the search for who did this. I don't give a damn if we anger the elders. They're getting to be yes-men to Swiftwater. He has some hang-up with you, but I'm not buying it. Do your thing, while we're doing ours. If you need backup, let me know. I'll be there."

Lani let go of the breath she'd been holding. "Thank you. I wasn't sure where you stood. It helps to know you haven't lost faith in me."

His eyebrows rose. "Are you kidding? You're the

best thing to happen to BLES. We needed fresh blood. Too many of us have gotten complacent. Now this..." He shook his head. "We've had people go missing, but never blatant murder. It's as if the killer wants us to find him but is leading us on a wild goose chase in the meantime. Why else dump the bodies where they can be easily found?"

"Agreed." Lani frowned. "So far though, I've not come across enough of a clue to feel like I'm heading in the right direction."

"Then dig deeper. I will be. Along with my shadow, the FBI agent," he said, wrinkling his nose.

"I'm going to follow Mark. Any idea where he might run to? Or does he have a favorite hangout?"

"I've seen him at the local bar on more than one occasion. You might try Mick's Bar and Grill. But don't bother getting there until after nine o'clock. That's when the hardcore drinkers congregate."

"Will you and the agent be there?" Lani asked.

"No. Everyone knows I'm on the case." The chief tipped his head toward Zach. "You and your fiancé could get in on the pretext of showing the new guy the local haunts." He grinned. "By the way, congratulations on your engagement. I didn't even know you had a boyfriend."

Neither had she. Lani's gut twisted. She didn't like lying to her boss. He'd given her a chance when others might have passed her over, since she was a female. "Thanks," she said. "I'll do my best."

The chief glanced over at Zach. "I trust you'll have her back?"

Zach nodded. "I will." He slipped an arm around Lani. "She can take care of herself but, sometimes, it helps to have eyes in the back of your head." He winked down at her. "I'll watch her back."

A shiver of awareness rippled across Lani's skin as she stared up into Zach's eyes. She'd like him to watch her back. Her *naked* back.

As soon as that thought popped into her head, her cheeks burned.

Zach's lips turned up on the corners.

Could he read her naughty thoughts? More heat spread up her neck and into her cheeks.

Her boss chuckled. "You two don't do anything I wouldn't. And if you do, use protection." He winked and slid into his service vehicle. "And let me know if you find anything we could use in our investigation."

Lani swallowed hard, turned to the chief and touched two fingers to her temple. "Yes, sir."

Chief Black Knife drove away, his SUV bumping across the road leading toward the highway and pavement.

"Ready?" Zach asked.

Oh, she was ready...but he didn't need to know for what. Her thoughts were headed into dangerous territory. Territory she had no business wandering into. Zach was on a temporary assignment.

Her.

He wasn't there to scratch the itch he'd created the first time she'd tackled him in Afghanistan.

ZACH HELD the truck door for Lani, though he knew she could do it herself. She was the tough cop who could take down a felon twice her size and pin him to the ground. Still, she was all woman beneath the badge.

She'd sparked his interest in Bagram. He'd thought it was a passing desire. After redeploying to the States, he'd found himself thinking about the Blackfeet beauty and wondering what she was doing. Had she redeployed? Had she gotten out of the military and returned to Montana as she'd said she would? Though he'd given her his cellphone number, Zach hadn't expected to hear from her ever again.

When her call had come through, he'd been more excited than he'd thought he could be over a woman he'd met while deployed. It wasn't as if they'd slept together, or even kissed. He'd found her fascinating. Her background similar to his and her dedication to helping others made him want to know her even more.

"Where to?" he asked as he drove away from the dilapidated trailer.

"The diner." She glanced his way. "I don't know about you, but I'm hungry, and we have time to kill until going to the bar tonight."

"Is the diner like most diners in a small town?" Zach asked.

"You mean, places where everyone eventually goes, and coffee and gossip flow freely?" She grinned and nodded. "Yes. We might learn something more while we eat."

Zach loved it when Lani smiled. Her entire face brightened. She went from the focused, consummate professional cop to a young woman who was approachable and very desirable.

By the time they'd reached the asphalt road, all Zach could think of was how much he wanted to kiss Lani's full, luscious lips.

He had to shake himself as a reminder he was on a mission to protect this woman, not make love to her.

And, just like that, the thought of making love to Lani filled his head. When they'd been at Bagram, he'd seen her jogging in her PT shorts. Her long, slender legs with their well-defined muscles had made his mouth water and his groin tighten. The memory was just as impactful. He could imagine those legs wrapped around his waist. It was just as well they were headed to a public place, not back to her little cottage where they'd be alone.

Coffee and food would help get his mind off Lani's tight body and kissable lips.

At least, he hoped it would.

Minutes later, they were back in Browning. Zach pulled into the parking lot of the diner and turned off the engine. The lot was packed with vehicles. He glanced at the clock on his dash and noticed it was already six-thirty. "I didn't realize it was getting so late. We completely missed lunch."

Lani snorted. "I miss lunch more often than I remember it."

Which accounted for the fact she was slim, almost too skinny. "Remind me to get groceries when we're done here. I'm pretty good in the kitchen."

"The man can cook, fire an M4A1 rifle and rescue a damsel in distress." She nodded, a smile tugging at her lips. "I'd say you hit all the qualifications of a knight in shining armor."

"I haven't rescued you yet," he reminded her. "And shiny armor makes too easy a target."

"No, you haven't rescued me yet, but you're keeping me safe and helping me investigate the murders. I'd say that checks that box."

He shook his head. "Hold your judgment until I prove myself...in the kitchen, on the range and having your back. In the meantime, let's get some chow. I'm starving." He dropped down from the truck and rounded the front fender.

Lani met him there. So much for chivalry. He'd open her door for her, but she was quick and opened her own damned doors.

Zach found himself a little irritated. He wasn't a knight. He hadn't done anything extraordinary for her, and he didn't like taking credit for anything he hadn't accomplished. The best he could do, for now, was make certain she didn't get hurt and help her find the killer. Only then could he prove his worth as her protector and a valuable asset to Hank Patterson's Brotherhood Protectors.

He beat her to the door of the diner and opened it for her, giving him a smidge of satisfaction.

Inside, a waitress with dark eyes and a long black braid hanging down the middle of her back yelled out, "Find a seat. Menus are on the table. I'll be with you in a moment."

Lani led the way, selecting a booth in a corner. She sat with her back to the wall, her gaze on the door.

Zach fought a grin. The woman was Old West. He bet that if she played poker, she'd have her pistol on her lap, her hand on the grip.

Zach sat across from her, turning slightly sideways in the seat to give him more of a view of the rest of the diner's interior. He could also keep an eye on the door in his peripheral vision. He lifted a laminated menu from where it was wedged between the napkin holder and the salt and pepper shakers.

"Hi, Lani." The waitress who'd yelled at them arrived at the booth, a pot of coffee and two mugs in her hands. "Coffee? Or does it keep you up at night?"

"I'll take a cup," Lani said.

"Make that two," Zach seconded. He'd need it to stay awake later that evening at Mick's Bar and Grill.

The waitress plunked the mugs on the table and filled them with coffee.

The heavenly scent filled Zach's nostrils. He inhaled deeply.

"Cream?" she asked.

"Black," Lani said at the same time as Zach. She laughed as she met his gaze. "I learned to drink it black when I was deployed. Faster, easier and more consistent. We couldn't always get cream."

"I started drinking coffee at the age of seven. Always black, no sugar." He lifted his mug and sipped the hot liquid.

"Careful," the waitress said. "It's hot."

He swallowed the steaming brew. "It's perfect."

She smiled. "You must be Lani's fiancé. I'm Rebecca."

"Zach," he offered.

"Nice to meet you," she said. "And I hear you're Blackfeet."

"A quarter," he corrected. "My grandmother was one hundred percent."

"Welcome to Browning." She held out her hand.

Zach set his mug on the table and shook the waitress's hand. "Nice to meet you, Rebecca."

The woman's cheeks pinkened. She pulled her hand free and fished a notepad and pencil out of her apron pocket. "What can I get you two to eat?"

"I'll have the usual," Lani said.

"One serving of pot roast." Rebecca jotted notes

on the pad then looked at Zach. "And you?"

Zach slid the menu back in its slot. "I'll have the same."

The waitress left to place their order with the kitchen, deliver plates of food to another table and refill water glasses on other tables.

"Rebecca is raising two children on her own and going to college part time," Lani said, her gaze following the other woman around the restaurant. "She has a big heart and a lot of determination. She'll realize her dreams, while setting a great example for her kids."

"She's a woman to be admired," Zach said. "My mother raised me on her own. She worked a couple jobs to make ends meet and keep a roof over our heads."

"Where is she now?" Lani asked, her attention shifting to Zach.

His lips thinned, and he stared down into his half-empty coffee mug. "She died of breast cancer, right after I graduated from high school."

"I'm sorry."

He shrugged. "It was a long time ago."

She reached across the table and took his hand. "It's hard to lose a parent at such a young age."

He curled his fingers around hers, liking how warm and strong they were. "I joined the Army after the funeral. I couldn't stay in my hometown."

"Where was your hometown? I know you said

you were from Montana, but where in Montana?"

"I grew up in Great Falls," he said.

"About two hours from here."

He nodded. "Your determination and desire to return inspired me to come home. I figured it was time to come back and see if there was anything left to keep me here."

She squeezed his hand. "I hope you stay. The state needs its children to come home. Only those who were born and raised here understand how deep the rivers run, how blue the skies are and how tall the mountains stand."

"I hadn't been back since my mother's passing." He smiled across the table and curled his fingers around hers. "And you're right. This place is still in my blood."

"I've found it to be more than just a place. It's the air I breathe, the beat of my heart and my state of mind." Her gaze met his. "No matter the people who aren't here anymore. It's home."

"You two are too cute," Rebecca's voice jerked Zach out of the depth of Lani's eyes and back to the diner. "I can come back while you share a moment..." The woman held two plates of steaming hot roast beef, potatoes and carrots.

Lani pulled her hand free of Zach's, her cheeks flushing a warm red. She leaned back. "No, please. We're starving."

Rebecca chuckled. "I get that, but I'm not so sure

you're starving for food." She winked as she laid the plates in front of Lani and Zach. "I'll be right back with your dinner rolls and a refill on the coffee."

Zach used the time it took for Rebecca to duck back into the kitchen to gather his wits and focus on the food in front of him. For a moment, he'd completely lost himself in Lani.

Her passion for and commitment to life in Montana were as infectious as her smile and laughter. He couldn't help but feel the same when she was around. Thus, his decision to return to Montana, a state he'd associated with loss and sorrow. It was if she'd thrown off the pall of death and opened the curtain of life so that he could once again see the big blue skies and the frosted tips of the mountains in the distance. Suddenly, he remembered the good times of his youth, the camping trips, canoeing the rivers and fishing in the lakes. His mother had loved Montana as much as Lani. She'd taken him across the length of the state, showing him the beauty of the plains to the stunning mountains and the ancient glaciers.

Rebecca returned with a basket of dinner rolls and the pot of coffee. She topped off their mugs and stood for a moment, smiling at them. "It's good to see young people in love."

Lani's cheeks pinkened again.

"Have you picked a date yet?" she asked.

Zach shook his head. "I only just asked her."

"Show me the ring," Rebecca held out her hand.

Lani twisted the ring on her finger and held out her left hand, her gaze shooting across to Zach.

He winked.

"Wow. That's a big rock." She held Lani's hand in hers and studied the ring. "He must love you a lot."

Zach nodded. "Yes, I do. She's everything I ever dreamed of. I still can't believe she said yes."

Rebecca cocked an eyebrow. "Seriously? Have you looked in the mirror lately?" Then she chuckled. "Lani, sweetheart, he's a keeper. If you decide to ditch him, give me a little head's up." Her smile faded. "Really, you two look like you're made for each other." She let go of Lani's hand. "We needed a little happiness around here after what happened last night."

Lani nodded, tucking her hand in her lap. "You heard?"

"About Tyler and Ben?" Rebecca nodded. "I can't believe they're dead. They were good people. They didn't deserve to die like that."

"I stopped out at Ben's place to give my condolences to Mark," Lani said, lifting her fork, her gaze on her food.

Rebecca snorted. "Was Mark even lucid enough to understand what you were saying?"

Lani shook her head. "I didn't get to say anything to him. He lit out like his tail was on fire."

"Idiot. Probably cooking meth or something,"

Rebecca said, shaking her head. "Ben tried to get him to quit the drugs. He was fighting a losing battle with that one."

"He left so fast…" Lani shook her head. "I worry he'll hurt himself. I wish I could find him and make sure he's okay."

"He'll probably head back to their trailer when he sobers up," Rebecca said.

"I doubt it. Black Knife confiscated his stash. He's probably afraid he'll be picked up for possession with the intent to sell."

"Serve him right. Might do him some good to spend some time in jail. He could stand some solitude to detox," Rebecca said.

"Besides the trailer he shared with Ben, does he hang out anywhere else?" Lani asked. "I'm really worried about him."

Zach almost grinned at the concern on Lani's face. After Mark had knocked her down, she was probably more concerned about taking the bastard down and forcing some information out of him.

"You gonna haul him in if you find him?" Rebecca asked.

"Not unless he wants me to," Lani said. "I want to make sure he's okay. Losing his brother had to hit him pretty hard."

Rebecca shook her head. "Ben tried so hard to get him straight. Doesn't make sense that Ben died, and Mark is still alive."

"I know what you mean," Lani said. "Any idea where I can find Mark. I think Ben would want someone to check on him."

"If he's afraid to go home, he might have holed up with one of his druggie friends. I think some of them hang out at the old abandoned warehouse. You know, the one on the north side of town, out toward the grain silo."

Lani nodded. "I've chased teens out of there. Sometimes, they go out there to drink and raise hell."

"Damned dangerous, if you ask me," Rebecca said. "They say the floors are rotting, and when the wind blows through the cracks in the wall, it sounds like screaming banshees." The waitress shivered. "Wouldn't catch me out there after dark. Place gives me the creeps."

A customer called for the waitress.

Rebecca grimaced. "Duty calls. Let me know if you need anything." And she was away to help her other customers.

Lani dug into her food and lifted a forkful up to her mouth. "Lou makes the best pot roast in Glacier County." She popped the bite into her mouth and moaned. "Amazing."

Zach's groin tightened. He could imagine that same sound coming from her mouth in the middle of making love. Shifting in his seat, he forced a chuckle. "You make eating so interesting."

She tipped her chin toward his plate. "You haven't

tried it."

Lifting his fork, he placed a bit of the roast in his mouth. The explosion of flavor left him moaning as well.

Lani laughed. "Told you."

He was entranced by her laugh as much as he was by the melt-in-his-mouth roast beef. "I concede. You're right. The roast is out of this world. I can't believe I had to come all the way to Browning, Montana, to find it."

"See? It's not all boring on the rez," she said. "We have our perks."

"Like Lou's pot roast." Zach glanced toward the kitchen where he could see a man with his hair pulled back in a ponytail, placing a plate on the ledge for the waitress. "Remind me to compliment the chef."

"He'd like that," Lani said and popped a bite of potato into her mouth.

After another mouthful of the delicious meal, Zach asked, "Where did he learn to cook like that?"

Her lips lifted on the corners. "In the Navy. He cooked for the crew of an aircraft carrier."

"That's a tough audience."

Lani nodded. "He was selected to cook for the President of the United States, but Lou chose to return to Browning, instead."

"That he was selected was a huge honor," Zach said. "I'd heard they sometimes take the best of the

Navy's best cooks to function as chefs for the White House."

Lani nodded. "Instead, Lou came home, bought the diner from the previous owner and started cooking for his people. He also volunteers on his days off doing home repairs for some of the families living in substandard housing."

"He and Rebecca better watch out. If the killer is targeting do-gooders, they might be next on his list."

A frown pulled Lani's brow downward. "They are good people. And there are so many more." She laid her fork on the table, her food only half-eaten. "We have to find the killer before he targets someone else."

"Agreed. And to do that, you need energy to keep you going late into the night." He tipped his head, indicating the food on her plate. "Eat."

Slowly, she lifted her fork and pushed a cooked carrot around on her plate. "I feel like I should have been there for Tyler and Ben."

Zach shook his head. "Lani, you didn't know someone was going to kill them. You can't be everywhere, all the time."

"I know, but it happened on my shift."

"You didn't kill them. You can't take the blame."

"But I've sworn to protect the people on the reservation." Again, she set her fork down next to her plate, her brow furrowing.

Zach tried another tactic. "If you don't eat all your

food, you're going to upset Lou."

"I'll take it to go and finish it another time." She looked up, her gaze searching the diner.

Rebecca hurried over. "What's wrong? Did the food get too cold? I can warm it up for you."

Lani gave Rebecca half a smile. "No. It's good, as usual. I'm just full. Can I get a box to take it home in?"

"Sure." She turned to Zach. "You too?"

He nodded. Though the roast was good, he too had lost his appetite. "Please."

The waitress left, returning with the boxes and their check.

Zach pulled out his wallet and paid the bill before Lani could.

Rebecca took the money to the register.

"But you're working for me. I should be paying the bill," Lani insisted, keeping her voice low so that Rebecca couldn't hear her protest.

"You introduced me to the best pot roast since my mother's." He grinned. "It's on me."

Rebecca returned with his change and a smile. "It was really nice meeting you, Zach." She gave him a quick hug.

"Nice to meet you, too," Zach said, surprised by the outpouring of warmth from a veritable stranger.

The waitress brushed a tear from the corner of her eye. "You make me believe in love again. I don't think I've seen Lani happier."

CHAPTER 6

Rebecca leaned forward, wrapped her arms around Lani and squeezed her tightly. "I wish you two a wonderful life together. You deserve to be happy."

"Thank you, Rebecca." Lani's cheeks burned. She hated lying to Rebecca about her engagement. The woman was her friend and deserved all the happiness she was wishing on Lani and Zach. "You deserve the same."

Rebecca laughed and looked to Zach. "You don't happen to have a brother, do you?"

Zach lifted his shoulders and let them fall. "Sorry. I'm an only child."

"It doesn't hurt to ask," Rebecca said. "Have a good night."

"Be safe," Lani said. "Have someone walk you to

your car after work, and don't stop to pick anyone up on the road."

Rebecca frowned. "You think I might be a target?"

"We haven't found the killer yet," Lani said. "I'd advise everyone to do the same. Until we find him, don't trust anyone."

The waitress nodded. "I hate that we have to be so distrustful."

Lani squeezed Rebecca's arm. "Me, too." She gathered the two boxes of food and turned toward the door.

Zach slipped an arm around Lani's waist and guided her to the exit.

She liked the way his arm around her felt so natural and exciting at the same time. She found herself wishing he really was that into her and would continue to wrap his arm around her, but because he wanted to. Not because it was part of their cover.

Outside, he opened the passenger door of his pickup and took the boxes from her. Once she'd climbed in and fastened her seatbelt, he handed her the boxes.

"We have enough time to take this food to my house," Lani said.

Zach left the diner and started to turn toward Lani's house on the southern corner of town.

"Before we go to my house," Lani said, "let's swing by the abandoned warehouse. I want to see if anyone's hiding out there."

"You mean Mark?" he asked.

Lani sighed. "Or anyone. We don't know that Mark is the killer. But I'd really like to ask him questions about who Ben might have had contact with."

"Which way?" Zach asked.

She turned her head toward the right. "Head north."

Zach pulled out onto the main street, cutting through Browning and heading toward the north.

Lani scanned the streets, searching the faces of people standing on corners, sitting on their porches or strolling in the evening dusk as the sun sank below the mountain peaks in the distance. It should have been a picture of an idyllic life. Instead, she tried to see behind their stares or casual waves. Was one of them the killer, hiding behind a friendly façade?

"I hate thinking any one of them could be smiling as they plot the death of his next victim," Lani murmured.

"Until we find the killer, you have to think that way. If you don't, you might be the next one on his list."

Lani nodded. "I know. And I'm keeping vigilant. But I don't have to like having to treat every person in town like a potential killer." She looked over at him. "I mean, what if it was Rebecca or Lou? I would be just as surprised as Ben and Tyler. I saw their bodies. Neither had any defensive wounds on their hands or arms. They didn't know they were about to die."

"I doubt it was Rebecca. Although she looks physically fit, she couldn't have lifted Ben or Tyler into a vehicle, and then carried Tyler up steps into a trailer to dump his body."

"True. But Lou is certainly strong enough to do all that." She shook her head. "I just can't see some of these people being cruel enough to kill. Most of them are just trying to eke out a living to feed their families." She raised her hand. "And before you ask, both Tyler and Ben still had their wallets in their pockets, with all their money and credit cards intact."

Zach's lips twitched. "I wasn't going to ask. But thank you. At least, now, I don't have to wonder."

"Sorry." She gave him a crooked grin. "Sometimes, I jump ahead and anticipate questions." She looked at the road ahead. "Turn left here."

He made the turn and drove several blocks. The road ended at an abandoned warehouse that rose two stories. Some of the siding had been stripped away, and several sheets of metal roofing were either missing or peeled back by the wind.

"Some of the building's materials have been removed by people who live on the reservation to patch exterior walls of the homes they live in," Lani explained. "The reservation council had a fence built around the site to keep people out because it was just too dangerous. And it was less expensive to put up the fence than to tear down the building." She nodded toward a gap in the fence. "Fences don't always keep people out."

Zach shifted his truck into park.

Lani set the food boxes on the console and climbed down from the truck, meeting Zach at the barrier in front of them. She slipped through the gap someone had cut in the chain link fence and walked toward the warehouse.

Zach ducked through the fence and caught up to her, pulling his gun from the holster beneath his jacket. "I don't like this."

Lani drew her weapon as she neared the building. "You don't have to go in. I just want to see if anyone has been squatting here or is using the building to deal drugs."

"Let me go first...?" he asked.

"I'm a trained law enforcement officer. I can handle this," she insisted.

"I was hired to protect you," he argued. "Let me go first."

"I need you to cover me from behind. I don't want you killed because you were helping me."

Zach frowned. "This is messed up."

"Because I'm female?" She shot a glance his way, her eyebrows raised. "If I were Chief Black Knife, would you insist on going first?"

He hesitated before answering honestly, "No."

Her lips turned upward. "Then let me do my job."

His lips pressed into a thin line. "Then be careful."

"Always," she said and approached a gap in the exterior siding panels, waving him to get behind her. With her back to an existing panel, she peeked around the edge into the darkened interior, giving her eyes a chance to adjust to the limited lighting inside. When she could make out shapes in the shadows, she slipped into the building, sinking into the shadows. One step at a time, she carefully placed her feet in front of her, making her way across a wooden floor that had long since weathered and lost its rigidity. In several spots, the floor sank beneath her weight. She'd been told the warehouse had a basement beneath the original floor.

The wood creaked behind her.

"Zach?" she whispered.

"Right behind you," he said.

"Don't get too close. I'm not sure how much weight this floor can hold."

"Then don't go any further," he urged.

"Stay where you are. I'll be right back," she said and moved forward, pulling her cellphone out of her pocket and hitting the flashlight button on it. Holding it high, she shined it front of her and into the far corners. Nothing moved.

"No one here," Zach said behind her.

"I want to look for evidence of occupation. Depending on what I find, it might tell me how long it's been since someone has been here."

"These floors are dangerous," Zach said. He must have taken another step because the boards creaked.

"Seriously, you weigh more than I do. Don't come any deeper into the building," Lani warned.

"If I'm not close to you, I can't help you," he said. "Please, come back out."

"I need to know if anyone's been in here." She continued across the floor. In the far corner, she saw what appeared to be some kind of blanket or tarp, wadded up on the floor. As she neared it, she held her gun in front of her. Again, nothing moved.

Lani nudged the fabric with her foot. A rat scurried out from beneath it.

Startled by the creature, Lani gasped.

"What?" Zach called out. "Are you okay?"

She pressed a hand to her chest, where her heart beat so hard and fast she felt as though it would jump out of her ribs. "Sorry," she said, swallowing hard. "I disturbed a rat."

"Rats can be rabid," he said. A loud crack sounded from the vicinity of where Zach stood.

"What was that?" Lani asked, standing perfectly still, her heart lodged in her throat.

"The floorboards cracked beneath my weight."

"Please," she begged. "Don't come any further."

"Trust me, I won't. I almost fell through," he said. "I see another door around the side closer to you. You might want to come out that way. The floor on this side has been exposed to the weather for too long. I don't think it will hold up under much more weight. I'm backing out. See you around the other side." The floor on that side of the building creaked and groaned as Zach edged his way back out the way they'd come in.

Left alone, Lani swallowed a sudden rush of panic. She was a cop. A professional. She had a gun and her wits.

Squaring her shoulders, she brushed the blanket aside and stared down at crumbled food wrappings, a discarded syringe, cigarette butts, an empty green and white cigarette package and crushed beer cans. She picked up the cigarette package. They items appeared fairly recent. If not days then within the past week or two. She held her hand over the cigarette butts, but felt no warmth, nor did she smell lingering smoke.

She poked around more, looking into discarded crates and beneath a broken pallet for any signs of stashed drugs. When she'd satisfied herself that no one had been there that day and no drugs remained in sight, she headed for the door Zach had indicated. As she reached for the handle it shimmied beneath her light.

"Lani?" Zach called out, shaking the door though it didn't open.

"I'm here," she said, the reassuring sound of Zach's voice chasing away the residual panic she'd felt a moment before. Lani twisted the lock on the door handle and pushed open the door.

Zach reached in and pulled her out and into his arms. "Next time, I go in first," he said, holding her close, his chin resting on top of her head.

She wrapped her arms, her hands still gripping her gun and cellphone, around his middle and rested her cheek against his chest, listening to the rapid beat of his heart. "Were you scared for me?"

"Damn right, I was," he murmured, his breath stirring the hairs at her temple.

"I can take care of myself." She tipped her head up and looked into his eyes. The sun had long since set, leaving the sky a dull, dark gray as the fading light extinguished.

"I didn't like being so far away from you," he said. "I can't protect someone if they don't stay close."

"I'll remember that," she said. "I didn't get to explore the basement, but I did find some signs the place had been used fairly recently, if not today." She held up the cigarette package. "This looked fairly recent, along with some beer cans and a syringe."

"We can come back when we have more light to work with."

"I'll bring a flashlight next time," Lani agreed. "Let's go to my house."

Zach slipped his arm around her waist as he had done at the diner and led her back to the truck.

Lani didn't mention that there weren't any people

around. They didn't have to pretend to be in love. But she kept her mouth shut and reveled in the way his arm felt all warm and strong at her back. She could get used to having it there. She could get used to having him around on a permanent basis.

Too bad his assignment was temporary.

He helped her up into the truck and climbed in beside her.

Without having to be told, he made his way back through town and out to Lani's house.

Lani sat in silence, stealing glances toward Zach. She was looking at him when he pulled up to her house.

"What the hell?" Zach said, a frown pulling his brow low.

Lani turned to see what had caused him to curse and gasped.

Her cute little white cottage was marred with blood red paint sprayed in giant swaths over the siding, windows and door. Among the random slashes of red were huge letters, spelling one word.

NEXT.

ZACH CAUGHT her arm before Lani could get out of his truck. "Stay."

"It's my home," she said.

"Whoever did this might still be here." He gave her a stern stare. "Please. Just stay."

She frowned heavily and opened her mouth. Then she closed it and nodded. "Be careful."

Zach slid out of the truck, pulling his weapon free of the shoulder holster. He hurried toward the house. The front door had been forced open, the doorframe split into jagged edges. Easing it wider with the barrel of his gun, Zach entered.

As an Army Ranger, he'd been trained in clearing an enemy-infested building. Drawing on experience, he moved through the small house, going room to room, searching for intruders. The living room had been tossed, the sofa cushions ripped and tossed across the room. The refrigerator had been tipped over and lay on its side. The mattress on her bed had been slashed and red paint sprayed across the walls in broad strokes. The clothes from her closet had been ripped from their hangers, strewn across the room, and were also covered in paint.

Zach kept moving. When he'd ascertained there were no lingering threats inside the house, he exited through the back door, scanned the surrounding tree line and circled back around the front.

Lani pushed the passenger door open.

"All clear," he said.

"Good. Because I wasn't waiting any longer." She dropped down from the truck and walked toward the house, her pace increasing the closer she got, her eyes shining in the light from the porch. "Son of a bitch." Color rose like red flags in her cheeks.

Zach's blood boiled for her. He wanted to erase all the paint across her home.

Her house had been vandalized. The safe place she went to find peace and relaxation had been violated. Lani scowled at the writing on the wall and entered the house without slowing.

"Damn it. Damn it all to hell," she yelled.

Zach followed her inside, cringing at what he'd already witnessed but feeling her pain at having her things destroyed.

"Lani, they're just things. They can be replaced."

"I got some of those *things* on my travels. I might never go back to some of those places."

"They're just things."

"Damn it. They were *my* things." Her voice trembled as she held a uniform blouse doused with red pain and stared at the clothes strewn across the room. "He even ruined my uniforms."

"Grab what clothes that aren't ruined. You can't stay here."

"I have nowhere else to go," she said, her voice fading. "This was my home."

"When we're done at the bar tonight, we can go to Cut Bank or Conrad and rent a motel room."

She shook her head. "It's too far away from my people. I won't be here to protect them."

Zach gripped both of her arms. "Sweetheart, did you read the word on the front of the house?"

She nodded.

"*Next*. He's targeting you next. You can't stay here. He might come back to finish the job." He kissed her forehead. "I'm *not* going to give him the opportunity."

"If he can't come after me, who else will he take his anger out on?" She shook her head. "I can't leave. I have to stay here."

Zach wasn't going to win the argument. She was determined to stay on the reservation. "If you insist, we'll figure it out." He'd stand guard while she slept. He'd gone without sleep before. It wouldn't hurt him to do it again.

Lani tipped her head back and looked up into his eyes. "You don't have to stay."

"I'm going to ignore that comment." He kissed the tip of her nose, and then let go of her arms. "Okay, then. We only have about an hour before we need to get to Mick's Bar."

Lani dropped the uniform top. "What do you suggest we do?"

"Call your boss," Zach said. "Report this crime."

Lani pulled out her cellphone and dialed the chief of police.

A couple hours later, after Black Knife and several of Lani's counterparts had been through her house, dusting for fingerprints and taking pictures of the damage, Zach and Lani watched as they drove away.

Chief Black Knife frowned as he walked out on the porch. "I don't like this."

Lani snorted. "And you think I do?"

He gave her a stern stare. "Be extra vigilant." He glanced over her shoulder at Zach. "Watch her." And he left.

Silence fell over the little house.

"What now?" Lani asked.

Zach clapped his hands together. "First, you need to help me get your refrigerator upright."

They worked together to set to rights what they could and piled the destroyed items on the porch outside. Her bed was a complete loss, as were her sofa and chairs. Zach found a hammer and nails and did what he could to repair the damaged doorframe until he could get lumber to replace the split wood.

With a nail in one hand, he held the hammer ready to slam it into the broken doorframe.

Lani stood by watching.

He hoped he didn't hit his thumb instead of the nail head. He smiled at her. "Without a bed, where do you plan to sleep?"

"I can sleep on the floor," she said.

He wouldn't let her sleep on the bare floor. "I have a sleeping bag I keep behind the back seat of my truck," Zach said. "You can sleep in it."

Lani frowned. "What about you?"

He would love to share that bag with her but knew that if he did, he wouldn't be sleeping that night. And he wasn't sure she'd want him to sleep with her. His desire could all be one-sided. He'd be watching over her, making certain no one slipped past him to harm one hair on Lani's head. "Let's worry about that after we hit Mick's Bar." He hammered the last nail into the front door frame and tested the locking mechanism. It held. He glanced at her.

Lani standing nearby, holding a jacket draped over her arm. "We'd better get going."

"I'm ready." He unrolled his sleeves, shrugged into his jacket and held the door for her.

She hesitated before walking through. "You don't think he'll come back while we're gone, do you?"

Zach shrugged. "If he does, we won't be here. And I'll clear the house before we go back inside."

With a nod, she walked through the door and waited for Zach to close and lock it before walking out to his truck in the light from the porch.

The drive to Mick's Bar didn't take long.

"I hope the killer is here tonight," Lani said, her lip curling up on one side. "I'd like to thank him personally for redecorating my house. I always hated that sofa. And the bed was as hard as a rock. I needed a new mattress."

"I hope he does, too," Zach said. "I'd like to end this game of cat and mouse, once and for all." He didn't like that Lani was the next target. He'd do everything in his power to keep her safe, but they still didn't know who they were up against. Plus, he didn't have any idea from which direction the attack would come. What if he was focused on the wrong direction?

He slipped his arm around her and guided her through the door of Mick's Bar, praying he would be there for her, no matter what direction the attack came from.

CHAPTER 7

LANI STEPPED INTO THE BAR, blinking to let her eyes adjust to the dim lighting. She wished she could shine a spotlight through the interior to help her look at all the faces. She searched everyone she could see, hoping to spot Mark. All the while she looked at familiar and unfamiliar faces, she wondered if one of them was the killer.

Her hands bunched into fists. If the killer was there, she'd be ready. He'd been clear in the message he'd painted on her house. She was next.

Good.

At least others would be safe, and she would be ready when he struck.

All the tables were taken by customers drinking beer or whiskey or shooting the breeze with friends.

Gazes swung their way as Lani and Zach wove through tables and past booths.

With his hand at the small of her back, Zach urged her toward the far corner of the bar and the only empty stool they could find. From that vantage point, they should be able to see everyone in the establishment and anyone coming through the door.

"Sit," Zach said into her ear.

When she hesitated, he leaned closer and pressed his lips to her temple. "Make it look like we're on a date." He smiled and asked her in a louder voice, "What do you want to drink?"

"Whiskey on the rocks," she said.

His lips curled in a smile that made her knees weak, and warmth heated her core. She took him up on the offer to claim the stool and slid onto the smooth wooden surface, turning her back to the bar. Lani wished the smile wasn't just for show. If they weren't on a mission, would he smile at her like that? If he did, she'd melt into a puddle of goo. The man was sexy as hell. She'd recognized that fact the first time she'd taken him down and pinned his body beneath hers.

Her heart fluttered at the memory. Did he think about that day? Lani had. Often.

Mick, the bartender and owner of the bar and grill, took Zach's order of one whiskey and one draft beer. A moment later, he had both drinks on the bar in front of Zach.

Lani lifted her glass to Zach. "To…us," she said.

He touched the rim of his to hers. "To us," he repeated, firmly, his gaze locking with hers.

Lani downed a healthy swallow of the clear amber liquid, feeling the burn all the way down to her stomach. Moments later, she felt her muscles relax slightly. Not so much that she'd be useless in a bar fight. Her focus became clearer. She smiled and set her glass on the bar. She didn't need another swallow. "I'm ready," she whispered.

Zach chuckled and took a long draft of his beer. "For what?"

"Anything."

Zach set his beer on the bar and draped an arm over her shoulder, leaning into her. "Have I told you how sexy you are when you go all cop?"

Butterfly wings erupted in her belly. Electricity shot through her where Zach's arm rested on her shoulders, his hand falling to hover over her breast. If she moved just a little, or drew in a deep breath, his fingertips would touch her there.

She caught herself drawing in a deep breath and let it out before her chest swelled. What was she thinking? They were there to find Mark and catch a killer. This was not a real date.

If it was, they wouldn't be in a seedy bar. They'd be at a nice restaurant, staring across a table at each other, probably holding hands. She'd like that. After a satisfying meal, they'd end up at her place where they'd close the door and make love against the wall because they couldn't wait to get to the bedroom.

Her pulse quickened at the mental picture she'd created. With Zach standing so near, she could smell his aftershave, the same brand he'd used in Afghanistan. She hadn't forgotten how much she'd liked it then. It was even more enticing now.

Focus.

Lani shook herself and forced her gaze to scan the room, searching for Mark. As she looked, she paused on each of the familiar faces, wondering if a killer lurked behind smiles and laughter.

Zach brushed his lips against her earlobe. "Do you know all these people?"

She smiled and nodded. "Most of them. Take the man with the long black hair tied back in a ponytail. That's Teddy Hunting Horse. Not only is he Chief Hunting Horse's brother, he also raises cattle and works part-time at the feed store. He has a wife and four kids. He's always there when someone needs a helping hand. The man beside him is James Matson. He works for one of the large ranching conglomerates outside the reservation. They share ranching tips and tricks."

"What about the three men at the table beside them?" Zach asked.

"David Two Ponies, the man with the Seattle Seahawks baseball cap, runs an auto repair shop in Browning. The two men with him are mechanics who work for him. They come here to blow off steam after a long day." She nodded toward a young man, wearing a hooded sweatshirt and jeans, sitting at a small table by himself. "The guy in the hoodie is Alan Swiftwater."

Zach frowned. "Wouldn't happen to be related to the tribal elder, would he?"

Lani nodded. "His son. He's been in and out of trouble all his life. I'm not sure what's going on with him, but he seems to think he's above the law because of his father's position. Either that, or he's pushing all of Daddy's buttons, trying to get his attention. He was suspended from school so many times his father finally let him finish by taking his GED. Ray sent him off to Great Falls to start college but quit funding him when he didn't show up for classes for an entire semester. Without money, he had to return to the reservation."

"Or get a job."

"He didn't have any real skills. His father was able to get him on at the feed store part-time." Lani sighed. "It's young people like Alan I'm trying to get through to. There are jobs and career paths if you're willing to put in a little work to get them."

A movement out of the corner of her eye brought Lani's attention to the front entrance. She stiffened.

In response, Zach's arm tightened around her shoulders. "What?"

"Mark," she said softly. "He just walked in. Block

me a little. I don't want him to see me until he's well inside the bar, and I can get to him quickly." Lani leaned back enough that Zach's big body stood in the way of her and Mark who hovered at the door, his gaze scanning the room.

The man had dark circles beneath his eyes, his dark hair hung lanky and dirty around his shoulders, and he looked like he'd slept in his clothes...in a pig's sty.

"He looks awful," Zach said.

"That's what drugs will do to a person." She sighed. "I've seen it all too often. It broke Ben's heart that he couldn't convince his brother to get clean."

"He's moving," Zach said.

"Which way?" Lani braced herself, ready to run after the man if he decided to make a break for it.

"Toward the other end of the bar." Zach turned sideways enough that Lani could see Mark lean against the counter and request a drink.

While he waited for his order, Mark turned his back to the bar and studied the occupants of the room, his gaze sweeping through until it came to the other patrons at the bar.

Lani ducked behind Zach. "I'm positive he didn't see you when we went to his trailer. Hopefully, he doesn't know you're my fiancé."

Mick set Mark's drink in front of him. As the bartender turned away, Mark leaned toward him, spoke and tipped his head toward Lani's end of the bar.

Zach stiffened. "They appear to be looking this way."

Mick said something to Mark.

Lani slipped off the bar stool, ready to sprint for the exit.

Mark's eyes narrowed. He slapped a bill on the counter, took one long draw from his drink, set it back on the counter and bolted for the door.

"He's running," Zach said.

Lani had already seen what was happening. She pushed past Zach and dashed for the door.

At the same time, David Two Ponies and his mechanics rose from their table.

Working her way around the three men, Lani continued on toward the door, only to be slowed again when Alan Swiftwater decided it was time to leave as well. He pushed his chair out from the table, effectively blocking Lani's way. "Officer Running Bear, I didn't expect to see you here. What brings you out this late? Are you working?"

"No," she answered, trying to look around him without being obvious. Mark was almost to the door.

"She's on a date," Zach said behind her. "If you'll excuse us, Lani isn't feeling well."

"Oh, sure."

When Lani stepped one direction, Alan stepped that direction. "Oh, sorry."

Again, Lani chose the other direction.

Alan sidestepped again, blocking her path. "There we go again. Tell you what…" He pointed to her right. "You go that way, and I'll go the opposite."

Mark had left the building by the time Lani finally made her way around Alan. She bolted for the door, having to weave her way through more tables and people.

Zach was right behind her as she blew through the door and out into the cool night air.

Stars shined down on the town of Browning, making it easy to see movement, but no matter which direction Lani looked, she didn't see Mark anywhere. She could barely hear the distant whine of a motorcycle engine. It was too far away to tell in which direction it had gone.

Lani blew out an exasperated breath. "Well, that was a bust. Next time, I'll have to find a place to stand that's closer to the door."

Zach nodded. "The place was pretty crowded."

David Two Ponies and his gang piled out of the bar, laughing and joking. David nodded a greeting to Lani and climbed into his truck. His mechanics climbed in with him.

Alan Swiftwater ambled out of the building, shaking a cigarette out of a green and white package. He placed it between his lips, glanced her way, and then turned and walked toward his bright red, beautifully restored 1967 Ford

Mustang, his shoulders hunched, his hood pulled up over his head, likely to block a cool northerly breeze. He climbed in and spun his wheels, leaving the parking lot and kicking up gravel in his wake.

"We might as well call it a night," Lani said. "I'll check Mark's place again in the morning. Maybe he'll have gone home by then."

Zach helped her up into the truck and climbed into the driver's seat. He turned the truck south and covered the short distance to her house in silence.

When they pulled into the driveway of her home, Lani sighed again. Nothing had changed. The paint was still splashed across the siding and her car. The pile of debris remained on the porch, untouched, a cruel reminder of the devastation they'd found inside the walls.

Feeling beat and a little discouraged, Lani dropped down from the truck and walked toward the house.

Zach got out, grabbed a rolled-up sleeping bag from behind the back seat of the truck and joined her before she reached the porch. He was first up the steps. Before she could get her key out, he tried the lock.

Lani was relieved the door was still in place, the lock having held. She used her key to let them in.

Zach dropped the bedroll on the floor, pulled out his gun and made quick work of clearing the rooms.

He was back in no time. "It's just as we left it," he assured her.

Glancing around the room, Lani wanted to cry. And she wasn't a weepy kind of female. She really must be tired to feel that way. "We still haven't established where you're sleeping," she reminded him.

"I'm not." Zach moved into the kitchen, flipped on the light switch and checked the interior of the refrigerator. "It's working."

Lani frowned. Zach was ignoring her concern over his sleeping arrangements. "You have to sleep sometime."

"I can go without sleep," he said. "I've done it many times."

Her lips pressed together in a tight line. "Maybe so, but you're not staying up all night on my account. If it makes you feel better, we can split the shift. I'll sleep the first four hours. Remember, I'm a cop. I've been working night shift. I'm used to being awake in the middle of the night."

"Okay." He gathered the bedroll and looked around. "Where do you want this?"

"Right here in the living room."

"You don't want it somewhere you can close the door?"

She shook her head. "Much as I hate to admit it, I feel safer when I'm in the same room as you." She glared at him. "Don't let that go to your head. I'll be fine once we catch this killer. In the meantime, I like

117

the company and the clear avenues of escape." She motioned toward the front and back doors.

And she liked him.

Now that they were alone, all the sexy thoughts she'd had about being with Zach came flooding back.

How was she supposed to sleep when all she could think about was getting naked in the sleeping bag with her protector?

ZACH SMILED. He was glad she'd chosen to sleep in the living room. "Good decision. I'd rather keep you within eyesight anyway." He untied the strings holding the roll tight and unfurled it onto the carpet.

Lani scrounged through a closet in the guest bedroom and found an undamaged pillow. She lay in the bag, turned onto her side and punched the pillow, wadding it up beneath her head. A moment later, she rolled to her other side and performed the same punching ritual. Then she lay still for an entire minute.

Zach held his breath. Had she really gone to sleep this time? He prayed she had, because he wasn't sure how long he could watch her wiggle and squirm without dropping down on the bag and holding her spooned in his arms.

Lani's eyes popped open, she sat up on the sleeping bag and wrapped her arms around her legs.

Zach chuckled. "You won't get much sleep sitting up."

She gave him a crooked grin. "I'm still wound up."

He did what he shouldn't have even considered and dropped down behind her. "Come here." He pulled her up against his body, stretched his legs out on either side of hers and massaged the back of her neck. "Better?"

"Mmm," she moaned. "Much."

Better for her, but not for him.

With her bottom rubbing against his crotch, his groin tightened, his cock pushing hard against the zipper of his jeans. Zach paused his massage to shift, trying to adjust for his purely physical reaction to being so close to this woman.

She leaned her head back and to the side to look up into his eyes. "Why did you stop?"

"There are some things better left unsaid." He grimaced and shifted again in his jeans. "You're doing crazy things to me."

"What do you mean?" Lani's brow puckered.

He moved forward, nudging her backside with the hard ridge beneath his jeans. "That's what I mean. I'm not a saint. And you're a very desirable woman." He bent to press a kiss to her forehead. "I think this is a very bad idea." He started to get up, but a hand on his thigh stopped him.

"Don't go," she said. She turned, facing him, still sitting between his outstretched legs, one hand resting on his thigh. "Did you really mean what you said?"

"What? That I'm not a saint?" He laughed. "You know from experience I'm not. You dragged my ass into confinement for fighting with that Marine."

"No, did you mean what you said...about me?" Her gaze captured his, and then lowered to his mouth.

"Oh, sweetheart, the part about you being desirable?" He drew in a deep breath and let it out slowly, trying to get his pulse in check. She had him tied up in a tight little knot of lust that could leave him completely unraveled. "Every word. You're a beautiful woman."

She looked at him as if he'd lost his mind. "I'm far from it. I'm plain. And I don't wear makeup or do my hair."

"You're not plain." Zach brushed his knuckles along her jaw. "Your skin is so soft and smooth. It makes me want to touch you all over."

She leaned into his hand.

He opened it to hold her cheek in his palm, and then swept his fingers through her hair. "And your hair is so silky and dark, like midnight." He cupped the back of her head. "Hell, I'm not a poet. All I know is that I haven't gotten you out of my head since you knocked me off my feet in Afghanistan."

"Seriously?" She chuckled. "I would have thought you'd be angry at having been bested by a female."

"I was, a little," he admitted. "But I deserved it. And meeting you was the best part of that entire incident." Zach brushed his lips across her forehead and down to her cheek. "Spending those few short hours with you changed my life." He raised his eyebrows. "I mean, I'm here, aren't I? I wouldn't have been able to answer your call if I'd remained on active duty. If I hadn't met someone as passionate about the state as you, I wouldn't have come back to Montana." His mouth skimmed across hers. "You reminded me of what I missed most about the state."

She tipped her head back, her eyes half-closed. "And what was that?" she whispered.

"The people, the beauty, the life." His mouth came down on hers, claiming her in a single kiss that burned through him like a brand.

Ever since he'd left the state, Zach had been searching for meaning for himself. He'd joined the Army to give him time and purpose on his journey. That experience had helped him to mature and make friends who were more like the brothers he'd never had growing up. But eventually, they were transferred to other units, deployed to other lands, separated from the military or killed.

He'd found a temporary home in the military. What he'd needed was a place to lay down roots. What he hadn't realized was that his roots had already been established. Right there in Montana.

He'd needed to live away from the state to understand what he'd left behind.

Being with Lani, there on the reservation that was her passion to serve and protect, made him aware of what he'd lost when he'd left the state. A part of himself.

He held her close, his tongue sweeping across the seam of her lips.

When she opened to him, he thrust past her teeth to claim her tongue with his in a long, sensuous caress.

Her arms wrapped around his neck, her fingers weaving into the hair at the back of his neck.

God, she felt good against him. Her long, lithe, muscular body fit perfectly with his.

Zach ran his hands over her shoulders and down her arms. He swept across her back, and lower, to cup her bottom in his palms. Then he laid her out on the sleeping bag and stretched out beside her, propping himself up on one elbow to better stare down at her and drink in her swollen, pouty lips.

"You're beautiful," he repeated.

When she opened her mouth to protest, he covered her lips with his own. "Don't argue. Accept that in my eyes, you are magnificent."

When he raised his head, she slipped a hand behind his neck and brought him back down to her, taking charge of the kiss, rising up to press her breasts to his chest.

He wasn't sure who started it, but one button loosened, leading to more, and soon, their clothes were flying off to the far corners of the living room until they both lay naked, the sleeping bag crumpled beneath them.

"I didn't mean to start something," he whispered against her ear as he leaned over her, nudging her knees open with his thigh.

She chuckled. "Too late to turn back now." She gripped his buttocks and guided him to her center.

When she increased the pressure, urging him to enter, he paused, a nagging voice in the back of his head making his brain engage. "Wait."

"Wait?" Lani moaned. "I can't wait." Her grip tightened.

"Protection," he said through gritted teeth. It was all he could do to hold back and think with his head, not his dick. He leaned over, snagged the jeans he'd tossed to the side and dug into the rear pocket, unearthing his wallet. After rummaging through the various slots inside, he gave a triumphant cry. "Thank God." Zach held up a single foil packet of protection.

Lani grabbed it from him and tore it open with her teeth.

"Hey, careful there, I only have two of these."

She grunted as she rolled it over his stiff erection, her fingers gliding down his length to cup his balls. "Don't make me wait any longer."

Zach laughed "Or what?"

"Or, I'll cuff you to my bedpost and have my wicked way with you," she said, her voice a low, sexy growl.

"Promises, promises," he murmured, his lips skimming across hers as he slid between her legs, his cock nudging her wet entrance.

Lani wrapped her legs around his waist and dug her heels into his backside, forcing him into her in one swift thrust.

"So much for taking it slow," he said as he eased back out.

Again, she clamped her heels into him and brought him back home, his cock filling her channel, sinking in the full length of him.

"Foreplay is overrated," Lani said. "I want you. Fast, hard and now."

Zach increased his speed, thrusting deep and hard.

Lani's legs unwrapped from around his waist and dropped to the floor, her heels digging into the carpet. For every one of his thrusts, she rose up to meet him.

The more he met her, the tighter his control stretched, until a burst of sensations jettisoned him over the edge. One last thrust, and he buried himself deep inside her, his shaft throbbing against the tight walls of her channel.

For a long moment, he held his breath, letting the

force of the orgasm wash over him. When he came back to earth, he dropped down on top of her and rolled her to her side, facing him. "Your turn."

She laughed. "I thought that *was* my turn."

"Oh, baby, you ain't seen nothin' yet. I'm going to make you roar like a lion before we're done."

Her brow puckered. "I'm not sure that's possible. Besides, I'm sleepy."

"Uh-uh." He traced a finger along her cheek and down the length of her neck. "It's your turn." His finger drew a path from the pulse beating wildly at the base of her throat down to the tip of her right breast.

"What if I can't...roar," she said, her voice fading.

Zach leaned up on his elbow and frowned down at her. "You've orgasmed before, haven't you?"

She shook her head. "Only when I've pleasured myself."

"No man has made you come?"

Her lips twisted. "Is that a bad thing?"

"Sweetheart, you deserve better." He smiled down at her. "Challenge accepted."

CHAPTER 8

LANI HAD LOVED every minute of having Zach inside her. Long ago, she'd believed the only way for a female to orgasm was to do it herself. None of her previous lovers had gotten her there. Not for lack of trying. They just never seemed to hit the right spot.

Lani lay back, fully expecting to be disappointed, yet again. But she didn't mind. Having Zach trail his fingers, lips and tongue over every inch of her would be just as satisfying. Wouldn't it?

He started with a kiss that set her world on fire. Then his mouth left hers and seared a path down the length of her neck to the pulse thumping against her skin at the base of her throat. He sucked and flicked that spot before moving on to her collarbone and lower to the first of her breasts.

When he flicked the tip of the beaded nipple, she

felt a tug deep down in her core. "Mmm. That's nice," she said.

He flicked it again, and then rolled it between his teeth.

It wasn't enough. Arching her back, she rose up, offering more of her breast.

He took it into his mouth, sucking hard. Again, that tug deep in her core made her writhe beneath him.

An ache grew, swelling inside.

Zach moved to the other breast and treated it to the same teasing nips and flicks, sucking it between his teeth.

He lay between her legs, his cock pressing against the inside of her thigh.

Lani wanted him inside again. She raised her hips, hoping he'd take the hint.

"Uh-uh," he said and abandoned her breast to burn a path of kisses into the skin over her ribs, down to her bellybutton. "Not until you get there, too."

Lani's breath caught as his hand cupped her sex and a finger found her wet entrance, pleasantly sore from his thorough lovemaking. He dipped a digit into her and swirled around, while his tongue flicked into her bellybutton then slipped lower to the curls hiding her clit.

He wasn't the first to go down on her. But she'd

never been quite so keyed up at this point. That ache that had started when he'd made love to her breasts had grown with each flick of his tongue.

She closed her eyes and willed him to continue, to take it a step further and touch her where only she had been able to ignite that flame.

He brought that wet finger up from her entrance, parted her folds and slathered the juices over that little strip of flesh all packed with a million little nerves just waiting to be set alight.

Then he stroked her with the tip of his finger.

Lani's hips rose automatically. He'd touched that spot. That incredibly elusive spot that lit her world.

He left her clit and dipped into her channel again.

Lani drifted back down, a little disappointed that the brief flick of his finger hadn't fully awakened her senses.

He was back with a wet finger and another attempt to get it right.

Zach swirled and tweaked with that magical finger, but he couldn't get it at just the right spot.

Lani shifted her hips, hoping to help him find it, but to no avail.

"Hey," he said, his breath warm against her sex. "Leave it to me."

She relaxed, determined to enjoy whatever he managed to inspire.

He moved lower between her legs, until his face was where his fingers had gone before. Parting her folds with his thumbs, he blew a warm stream of air over her heated flesh.

Lani sucked in a breath and waited. She had to watch, had to see him take her with his mouth.

And he did.

The first flick of his tongue tapped against the very tip of her clit.

A shock of electricity shot through her body.

She gasped, her body stiffening.

The second time his tongue touched her there, she slammed her palms to the floor and lifted her hips. "Please," she moaned.

He chuckled. "Please what?"

"Please, do that again."

He flicked her again. This time, he ignited that flame that exploded like a firestorm, sending heat-waves and electric shocks all the way through her and out to the very tips of her fingers and toes.

She would have been happy if he'd stopped there, but no. He increased his attack on her senses, laving, flicking and sucking her clit into his mouth until she was moaning, roaring his name in an attempt to capture the moment and save it for all eternity. Her release poured over her in waves, her body pulsing to the rhythm of his tongue moving against her.

When she thought she might never breathe again, she finally came back down to earth, the sleeping bag and the floor where she lay.

Zach climbed up her body, slipped a fresh

condom over his shaft and pressed it against her entrance. "Are you too sore to do it again?" he asked.

"No. Oh, no. Please." She tossed her head from side to side, still in a fever from the best orgasm she'd ever experienced. "I want you. Inside me. Now." She gripped his ass, guided him to her center and slammed him home.

He took her again, this time riding on the waves of her exquisite release.

Lani had never felt anything quite like it. She met his thrusts with her own, wanting him so deep that she couldn't remember where she ended, and he began.

When he came this time, his body shuddered inside hers, every one of his muscles so tight they were like steel bands.

Then he fell on top of her, rolled her onto her side and held her without breaking their intimate connection.

Lani lay in his arms, exhausted but replete, a smile curling her lips as she drifted into sleep.

"I love you," she whispered in her dream.

ZACH LAY FOR A LONG TIME, holding Lani in his arms, cherishing the moment, memorizing every curve of her delicious body. Somehow, he'd known it would be good with Lani. Never in his wildest dreams could he have known just how good.

The woman was as passionate making love as she was about everything else in her life.

As she'd drifted off to sleep, she'd murmured three words that had shaken him to his very core.

I love you.

He shook his head, even as he held her in his arms.

She'd been asleep when she'd said the words. They'd been part of a dream, not reality.

The words had poured over him like melted butter over pancakes, absorbing into every pore of his skin. If only she really did love him. What a life they could build together.

Images of a cottage with a picket fence and half a dozen dark-haired children running around the yard emerged in Zach's head. He'd never thought about settling down and raising a family. Hell, he'd only just gotten used to the idea of living in Montana again.

Lani shifted against him, nuzzling her cheek against his chest.

He liked the way she felt, how warm her skin was against his. He wanted that feeling to last.

A very long time.

As the air temperature decreased in the room, Zach knew he'd have to let go of her and wrap her in the sleeping bag. If he lay beside her much longer, he'd fall asleep. He couldn't let that happen. Not when Lani's life was at stake. That one word written on the exterior of the house had been seared into

Zach's memory. He couldn't let anything happen to this woman.

She had quickly found a way into his heart, and he wasn't ready to let her go.

Except to wrap her in the warmth of the sleeping bag, which he did, careful not to wake her.

He rose, dressed and checked the pistol in his holster. His gaze returned to the woman lying in the folds of the sleeping bag. She'd rolled to her back, the edge of the bag slipping low, exposing a full, luscious breast.

His groin tightening, Zach bent to cover the breast. He had to be vigilant. If anyone was going to attack, it would be in the dead of night, after they were both asleep.

Zach left Lani in the living room and made a cursory check of the other rooms, testing the locks on the windows. Back through the living room, he checked the lock on the back door and left the house through the front.

He checked his watch. Despite Lani's desire to take the second shift, Zach had let her sleep. It was nearing five o'clock in the morning. The sun would rise soon, and another day would begin. Another day of chasing leads. Why couldn't they catch a break on this guy? Who had it out for Tyler, Ben and, now, Lani?

Zach made a pass around the entire house,

checking for movement in the tree line or down the road leading up to the house. Other than a stray cat lurking in the woods, nothing moved. Clouds moved in, blocking the light from the stars, making the darkness even more complete, the only light now coming from the single bulb burning over the front porch.

He climbed the steps and had just reached for the doorknob when the door opened and Lani stood there, wearing only a T-shirt, her long legs bare in the light shining down over her.

She pushed the hair from her face and stared up at him. "You were supposed to wake me."

As she raised her arm to shove the hair back from her forehead, the hem of her shirt rose, exposing the curls over her sex.

Zach swallowed a groan. "Sweetheart, go back to bed. You're making me crazy."

She draped her arm over his shoulder. "Come with me."

"Someone has to keep an eye open for danger."

"Seems like we've made it through the night. What more could happen between now and sunrise?"

He backed her into the house, kicking the door shut behind him. "I'll tell you what could happen..."

Gripping her bottom, he raised her up, wrapping her legs around his waist. Then he leaned her back against the door and pressed into her.

"Mmm. I'm liking your scenario already." She leaned away from him, enough to reach down and unbutton the waistband of his jeans.

Zach took over, lowering his zipper.

His shaft sprang free.

"I don't have another condom," he said, nudging her entrance.

"That's okay," she said. "I have another idea. Put me down."

He lowered her until her feet touched the floor.

She didn't stop there but dropped to her knees and took him between her palms. "Your turn," she said with a smile.

Lani touched the head of his cock with the tip of her tongue.

The sensations shooting through him were so strong, he flinched.

Her chuckle sent heat through his soul. Lani wrapped her hand around him and stroked him all the way to the base of his shaft then rolled his balls between her fingers.

His groin tightened. He didn't think he could get any harder. "I won't last long with you doing that."

"I'm not done yet." She leaned forward and took him into her mouth, pressing his buttocks until he bumped against the back of her throat.

Zach gripped her head, his fingers threading through her long hair.

When she leaned back, his grip tightened, bringing her to him.

She took all of him again.

He couldn't just let her please him. He wanted to touch, feel and taste her, too.

Zach gripped her arms and raised her to her feet.

Lani frowned. "You didn't like that?"

He smiled through gritted teeth. "More than you can imagine. But I want to touch you, too."

"This was your turn."

"Why not make it both of our turns?"

"But you don't have another condom."

"We don't need one." He bent and swung her up into his arms.

Lani squealed and wrapped her arm around his neck. "Where are we going?"

"You'll see." He carried her to the living room and laid her on the floor. Then he stripped out of his clothes, pulled her shirt over her head and laid on the floor on his back.

His cock jutted straight out ready for more.

Sitting on the floor beside him, Lani wrapped her fingers around him and bent to claim him in her mouth.

"That's a start, but I want to taste you, too."

Zach positioned her hips over his face, one of her knees on either side of his head, and spread her legs until she'd lowered herself to within range of his mouth.

While she sucked his cock, he pleasured her clit.

Zach flicked and teased that highly sensitive area, sliding a finger into her channel. At the same time, he pumped upward into her mouth, her warm wet tongue swirling around him.

It wasn't long before he felt the surge of his release, and he fought to hold it in check.

Lani stiffened and sank lower over his mouth, her body bucking with her orgasm.

When he could hold it no longer, Zach pulled her off him and let go.

Lani stroked him, milking him until he was empty.

"Wow," she said. "That was better than coffee for waking me up." She rose to her feet and stretched her beautiful body. Then she reached down, extending a hand to him. "Come on. I'll wash your back, if you'll wash mine."

"Deal." He leaped up, slapped her bottom and raced her to the bathroom. Soon, they were laughing and covered in suds.

When they had thoroughly soaked the bathroom floor and used all of the hot water, they spent a long time drying every inch of each other's bodies, kissing and touching along the way.

After sopping up the water off the floor, they left the bathroom, dressed and threw the damp towels into the washer.

Zach was rolling up the sleeping bag when Lani's cellphone rang.

She was in the kitchen when she answered it. "Running Bear." She paused. "At home..." Lani listened. "He was at Mick's last night. No, I didn't get a chance to talk to him. He left in a hurry, why?" Her face paled. "Seriously?" She stared across the room at Zach. "At Kipps Lake? What time? Six? Where did they take him?" Lani nodded. "Yes, sir. I'll be there in five minutes." She ended the call, her gaze capturing his, her face pale and her eyes rounded. "They found Mark Wolf Paw's body in Kipps Lake this morning. It appears he drove his motorcycle into the lake and drowned."

Zach tightened the string holding the bedroll together and stood. "Suicide?"

"That's what it looks like." She frowned. "But as they pulled his body out of the water, Chief Black Knife noticed injuries to his forearms, as if he'd been blocking an attack. And there was a bruise at his temple."

Zach shook his head. "He was probably dead when he was thrown into the lake."

Lani nodded. "If he was murdered, at least we know for sure that Mark wasn't our killer. Someone might have killed him and staged it to look like suicide to make us think the killer is now dead."

"And we're back to square one," Zach concluded.

"Exactly." Lani pulled their dinners from the night before from the refrigerator and popped them into the microwave. "I need to get to the police station. The chief wants me fully engaged in the investigation again. He got the tribal elders to agree, finally."

"I don't have to eat. We can go right now," Zach offered.

Lani's lips twisted. "You might not be hungry, but that was quite the workout last night. I'm starving." The microwave beeped, and she pulled the food out, slapped the roast beef from her box between two slices of bread, grabbed a fork from a drawer, shoved her arms in a jacket and headed for the door. "I'll drive. You eat. I can eat mine on the way. I'm really good at eating on the go."

Zach took his food box from her, tossed her the keys and followed her out to the truck.

She climbed into the driver's seat and started the engine. After shifting into reverse, she took a bite out of her sandwich and backed out into the street. Then she shifted into drive and drove to the Blackfeet Law Enforcement station where several police and civilian vehicles were parked in the lot.

"Looks like we're late to the party," Lani said, taking another bite out of her sandwich.

Zach set his box on the dash, untouched. "Let's find out what we've missed."

"I wish we could have caught Mark last night. I just bet he knew something."

"Yeah. And he took that something to his grave." Zach met her at the front of the vehicle.

Lani was just eating the last bite of her sandwich.

He grinned.

She frowned. "What?"

Zach brushed a crumb from her chin. "I've never seen someone polish off a sandwich as fast as you just did."

Lani snorted. "You learn to eat and run. Hell, I learned that in Basic Combat Training. If you didn't get it down in three minutes, you didn't eat."

"I remember." He laid a hand at the small of her back. "Let's do this."

Though she was a cop in the middle of a murder investigation, Lani still liked that Zach opened the door for her and touched her like she meant something to him. She hoped last night was an indication of just how much he was beginning to care for her. If it wasn't...she was in for some major disappointment.

Once the killer was caught, Zach had no reason to stick around. It would be a shame to lose the only man who'd ever managed to get her off. A real shame. Besides, she liked having him around. He was strong, protective and didn't mind that she was a cop. Not many men would be okay with her being in law enforcement. Zach had only known her in that capacity. And he didn't seem to mind. In fact, he seemed to admire her strength and the fact she could take him down.

Who was she kidding? Not many men would tolerate that part of her.

Why should Zach?

CHAPTER 9

ZACH FOLLOWED Lani into Blackfeet Law Enforcement station where a crowd of people stood around, some in uniform. Some not. He recognized the police chief, the FBI agent and Raymond Swiftwater, the elder who had an attitude about Lani.

Lani pushed her way through the people standing around until she reached her boss. She kept hold of Zach's hand, dragging him in behind her. "What's going on?"

Chief Black Knife tipped his head toward the elders. "We're dealing with the death of Mark Wolf Paw. The elders are concerned that no progress has been made on the first two murders, and now we have another."

"What are you doing about it?" Chief Hunting Horse approached her. "Why don't we have more people on this case?"

"If you recall," Black Knife reminded him, "the elders asked that I work with the FBI agent in charge of the murder investigation. No others from the BLES force were to be involved."

"Aren't we short-handed on the force?" Hunting Horse asked. "Isn't that why we asked that only the chief of police and the FBI get involved?" The chief turned toward Raymond Swiftwater. "Wasn't that the reason you asked to limit our own personnel's involvement?"

Swiftwater frowned. "That hasn't changed. We're still short manpower."

"And you've had me bench one of my best from the investigation," Black Knife said. "Officer Running Bear has taken it upon herself, on my authority to continue investigating the murders of Tyler Light-foot and Ben Wolf Paw. On her own time."

Elder Swiftwater glared at Lani. "She was not to be involved in this case."

"Why?" Chief Hunting Horse asked. "Seems we should have as many people as possible looking for this guy. Instead, we've had another murder take place. We cannot continue to lose people. These were our brothers, our friends and the future of our people."

"Then I have your permission to bring Officer Running Bear back on the case?" Black Knife asked.

Swiftwater's lips pressed into a thin line as if he

wanted to say something but was holding his words in check.

"Yes," Hunting Horse said. "Officer Running Bear should be included in the investigation. We cannot afford to lose another member of our tribe." The older man turned and left the building, followed by his entourage of elders and assistants.

When they were gone, Black Knife faced Lani. "Something I didn't tell the elders is that the station was broken into last night."

Lani gasped. "Was anyone hurt?"

The chief shook his head. "No, but they tried to get into the evidence room."

"And did they?" Lani asked.

"No."

"Did you store the confiscated drugs in that room?" Lani started around him.

The chief snagged her arm. "I sent most of it on to the state crime lab. I kept a small amount here, hoping to smoke out those desperate enough to make a move on it."

"Good thinking." Lani raised an eyebrow. "And did you catch him?"

"I had a camera on the evidence locker, but whoever broke in sprayed the camera lens with red spray paint."

Lani gasped. "Just like my house."

The chief nodded. "Like your house."

"So, you didn't even get an image of your thief?" Lani's shoulders slumped.

Zach wanted to pull her into his arms and hold her. He was as disappointed as she was, and it wasn't even his job to protect the people of the reservation. He'd been hired to protect her, alone.

"No images."

"Fingerprints?" she prompted.

Again, Black Knife shook his head. "No. And he got away with the little bit of drugs I had stored in the evidence locker. He cut the lock and forced open the door. No one saw him coming or going."

"Damn," Lani said, her shoulders falling.

"What do you know about Mark Wolf Paw?" the chief asked. "Besides the fact he had a lot of drugs hidden in his trailer. Who were his friends? Who did he hang out with?"

Lani shook her head. "I haven't been here as long as you have, sir."

The chief grimaced. "And I haven't been nearly as observant as I should be about the young people on the reservation, a fact I plan to rectify as soon as possible."

"As I told you," Lani said, "we saw Mark at Mick's last night. As soon as he saw me, he made a run for it. I didn't catch up to him before he disappeared."

"The FBI agent and I haven't made much progress on solving the murders of Tyler and Ben." Black Knife sighed. "I believe we've interviewed the same people and gotten nowhere. And you heard the elders, they want answers. Now."

"We can't give them answers if we don't have them ourselves."

"How did the guy get into the station?" Zach asked.

"The man on desk duty made a trip to the bathroom," the chief shook his head. "The thief jammed the door shut on the bathroom, sprayed the camera and broke into the evidence locker. He was out in under the five minutes it took for Payton to contact one of the officers on duty using his cell phone and get him there to unblock the door and let him out."

"Were there any tire tracks at the lake where Mark was found?" Zach asked.

"Other than his motorcycle's tracks…?" Lani added.

Black Knife shook his head. "It appeared as if someone swept the dirt leading up to the entry point into the lake. Not even a shoe print remained."

Lani pressed her lips tightly together, her brow furrowing. "I'd like to go back out to the Wolf Paw home and see if I missed anything, a list of names, a cellphone, anything. I'd also like to check with the coroner and compare the bodies of the deceased."

Zach realized how gruesome that sounded, but he was also interested in the similarities and differences in the three attacks. "Ready?" he asked, wanting to get started on the day's investigative activities. He

ELLE JAMES

was worried about Lani. If the killer made good on his threat, he would be looking for his opportunity to get to Lani.

Zach wasn't going to let her out of his sight for a minute.

They left the station and walked out to his truck. He scanned the buildings and shadowy alleys for movement. Just because the killer had beaten his victims to death didn't mean he wouldn't consider a less hands-on death for Lani. A well-placed bullet would take her out faster and more efficiently. Not that Zach was eager to see her murdered. He worried he wouldn't be fast enough, or ahead of the killer's thought process.

"I'll drive." He slipped into the driver's seat and shifted into reverse, pulling out of the parking space. "Where to first?"

"The Wolf Paws' place," Lani said, her gaze on the road ahead.

They drove through town and out the other side, taking the road where the isolated trailer was parked.

As they turned onto the ragged road leading up to the trailer, Lani gasped. "What the hell?"

Small puffs of smoke rose from the Wolf Paw brothers' home. Nothing was left but the caved-in siding, the melted tire that had been on the roof and a smoking pile of rubble.

She climbed out of the truck and circled the wreckage. "What the ever-loving hell?"

Zach joined her in front of the truck.

"It must have burned during the night," she said. "It was far enough out of town, no one saw it."

"There's nothing here, let's move on to the coroner's office," he suggested. "Which way?"

"The Glacier County Coroner's office is located in Cut Bank. On our way back through Browning, I'll call in this fire. While we're in Cut Bank, we can run down those kids who threatened Tyler while we're there." Lani held her hands out, palms up. "What else do we have to go on?"

Zach could hear the frustration in her voice. He felt it himself. What did it take to bust a case wide open and nail a killer? He wasn't a detective, and neither was Lani. She was working on a promise she'd made to a grieving grandmother.

The case had to break soon. He and Lani were living on the edge of disaster. It was only a matter of time before the killer made his move on Lani. Through every battle, Zach's instincts had proven themselves over and over. He could feel it in his bones. That time was coming soon.

AFTER LANI GAVE ZACH directions to the coroner's office in Cut Bank, she sat back in the passenger seat, running everything she knew through her thoughts but coming up with nothing. Not a damned clue that would lead her to Mark, Tyler or Ben's killer. Bodies were stacking up in Browning, Montana, and she didn't know where to turn next.

They pulled into the parking lot at the coroner's office and got out.

Lani had been there before on one other occasion. A dog had dug up bones by the river. They'd been taken to the coroner for identification. When they couldn't identify them, they'd turned the bones over to the FBI. A forensic scientist had determined the bones dated back to the late eighteen hundreds.

Inside the office, Lani asked to speak to the medical examiner. Martha, the woman at the front desk, asked her to wait while she asked whether he was available. He already had someone with him.

When she opened the door behind her to walk into the back room, Lani heard voices, one of which she recognized as Raymond Swiftwater.

Without waiting for the woman to clear their entry, Lani followed her through the door to the examination room where three bodies lay on stainless steel tables. Swiftwater stood beside one with the Medical Examiner. They both glanced in Lani's direction.

Martha spun and glared at Lani. "You can't be back here without the M.E.'s okay."

"I'm here for the same reason as Mr. Swiftwater," Lani said. "I want to know the status of Mark Wolf Paw's examination." She met Swiftwater's gaze with a direct one of her own.

The M.E. waved at Martha. "It's okay. Officer Running Bear can stay."

"What about him?" Martha tilted her head toward Zach.

"Are you with Officer Running Bear?" the M.E. raised an eyebrow at Zach.

Zach nodded. "Yes, sir."

"You can stay, too."

Martha huffed and left the room, giving Lani the stink-eye for not following the rules.

"Don't let Martha bother you," the M.E. said with the hint of a smile. "She's like a bulldog and runs interference for me when I'm really busy."

"Thank you for letting us stay," Lani said.

"No problem," he said in his soft voice. Lani had met the M.E. before. He'd been a family practice doctor before he'd left his practice and "retired" to the position of medical examiner and coroner of Glacier County. As he'd told her before, it was a lot less stress.

Lani and Zach joined the two men at the table.

Swiftwater shot a venomous glare at Lani and Zach before schooling his expression into one of disinterest.

"I was just getting started explaining what I've found so far," the M.E. said. "From what I can tell, Mr. Wolf Paw didn't die from drowning. I found no water in his lungs." He pulled the sheet back and lifted the deceased man's arm, turning it so that they could see the underside of the forearm. "You see these bruises? They were made before he died." The M.E. held his own arms up in front of his face. "Most likely, he was defending his face and head from an attack with a blunt weapon." He slid his gloved hand down to Mark's fingertips. "I also found skin and blood underneath his fingernails. In the struggle, he got a piece of his attacker. Whoever it was should have a pretty significant scratch on an exposed portion of his body, like his arm, face or neck." He lowered the arm and pointed to the side of Mark's head. "Most likely, he was killed by blunt force trauma to his skull here," he touched the man's temple where a blue bruise stood out, "or here." The M.E. parted Mark's dirty hair and pointed to a large lump on the man's scalp. "He was dead before he went into the lake."

"So, it wasn't suicide," Swiftwater stated.

"No," the M.E. said. "Either it was murder, or he had a big fight with someone and lost."

Swiftwater stared at the man lying on the table without displaying an ounce of emotion. "Thank you for your time," he finally said, turned and left the room.

Lani followed the man. "Excuse me, Elder Swiftwater."

The man stopped and turned. "Yes, Officer Running Bear?"

Lani crossed her arms over her chest. "Why are you here?"

Swiftwater lifted his chin. "As a tribal elder, I consider it my responsibility to know what's going on with the people of the Blackfeet reservation."

Lani's eyes narrowed. "Isn't visiting the coroner taking your responsibilities a little far?"

"My concern is for my people. Since the tribal police and the FBI can't seem to find the man responsible for now three deaths on the reservation, I've taken it upon myself to conduct my own investigation." The passion in his voice faded, and he added in a flat tone, "Someone has to stop the killer before he takes yet another life. Now, if you'll excuse me, I have work to do." Swiftwater's cellphone chirped in his pocket. He reached in and pulled it out, answering with a curt, "Swiftwater." He listened, frowning. "How the hell do I know?"

Lani observed the man's face go from no emotion to instant anger. "I told you...I don't know. He's a grown man; he has the schedule. It's up to him to get to work on time. Call his cellphone and leave me out of this." Swiftwater closed his eyes, a muscle ticking in his jaw. "I know it was a favor. I know you need the help, but I have no control over my son. Fire him, if that's what you need to do." Swiftwater pulled the phone away from his ear, jabbed his finger at the button ending the call and stuffed the device into his jacket pocket. He shot a glare at Lani, turned and left the coroner's office, letting the door slam closed behind him.

"Is he always that angry?" Zach said beside her.

"I don't know about others, but he always seems angry around me or his son." She couldn't imagine growing up around a father with such a sour disposition. She'd been fortunate to have a loving mother, who had supported and encouraged her to follow her dreams, wherever they led.

Zach touched his hand to the small of her back.

For a moment, Lani leaned into that hand and against Zach's shoulder. She missed her mother, and she was tired. Tired of hitting brick walls and tired of dead ends. "I wish the killer would attack me. At least then I would know who it was and could do something about it."

"I, for one, hope he doesn't attack you." His hand slipped around to hook her hip, pulling her closer. "He knows you don't know who he is and will have the advantage of surprise on his side. I suspect it's someone each of his victims knew and never suspected would attack them."

Lani glanced up into Zach's face. His jaw was firm, his gaze on the door that had closed a moment before. He was glad he was with her. Having another pair of eyes watching her back made her feel a little safer.

"I want to stop by the homes of the guys who bullied Tyler at the theater. I don't think they could have been on the reservation without being noticed, but it doesn't hurt to cover all the bases."

Zach nodded. "Let's do this."

Lani looked up the addresses of the three young people and typed the first into her map application on her cellphone. They arrived a few minutes later outside of a white house with antique blue shutters that looked as if it had been built in the early nineteen hundreds. "This is where Russell Bledsoe lives, or at least, where his parents live," she said.

Lani climbed out of the truck and headed for the front door.

Zach caught up as she rang the doorbell.

After several seconds, she heard a male voice inside yell, "I'll get it."

A young man with blond hair, blue eyes and broad shoulders like a football linebacker opened the door. "Yeah?"

"Are you Russell Bledsoe?"

He frowned. "I am. Why do you ask?"

Lani pulled her wallet out of her jacket pocket and flipped it open to her BLES badge. "I'm Officer Running Bear from the Blackfeet Law Enforcement Service. This is my assistant, Zachary Jones. Could we ask you a few questions?"

Bledsoe's frown deepened. "I don't know anything about the reservation. I haven't been on it since I was a little kid."

"We'd like to ask you about your relationship with Tyler Lightfoot."

He shook his head. "Was he one of the people who was in the news report?"

"What news report are you referring to?" Lani asked.

"The one about the three men murdered on the reservation?" Bledsoe offered.

Lani nodded. "Yes, Tyler was one of the victims."

"I never knew him or any of the others, personally."

"But you knew of them?"

Bledsoe shrugged. "I might have run into Lightfoot a couple of months ago here in town. And everyone knew Wolf Paw."

Lani's eyes narrowed. "Why did everyone know Wolf Paw?" She suspected the reason but wanted to hear it from someone other than a member of her tribe.

The young man shifted his weight from one foot to the other. "Well, everyone who wanted drugs knew him." Bledsoe held up his hands. "Not me. I'm clean. I've got a football scholarship. I'm not going to screw that up." He dropped his hands. "Wolf Paw was the guy everyone went to for their fix. He was dealing. In a big way."

Lani circled back to her original reason for coming. "Did you and your friends, Dalton Miller and Brent Sullivan, threaten Tyler Lightfoot outside the Orpheum Theater a couple months ago?"

The young man stiffened. "I don't know what you're talking about."

"Did you and your friends threaten Tyler Lightfoot because he was dating Natalie Preston?" Lani asked.

He started to shut the door. "I'm done talking here."

Lani placed her hand on the door. "Russell, where were you two nights ago around midnight?"

A woman appeared behind Russell. "He was here at home in bed. I can vouch for that. He'd been out with his friends earlier, but he was home early that night. You can subpoena his phone and social media records. He was in this house all that night."

"Mom, I can handle this," Russell said.

His mother shot him a narrow-eyed look. "You've said enough. Anything else will have to be with an attorney present." She stepped in front of her son. "Now, unless you have a warrant, I suggest you leave."

"Thank you, Russell," Lani said, capturing the young man's glance over his mother's shoulder. To his mother, she said, "For what it's worth, I don't think your son committed the murders. I just needed to ask him some questions so that I could cross him off my list of suspects."

ELLE JAMES

The woman responded by closing the door in Lani's face.

"Well, that was productive," Lani said, her tone dripping sarcasm. "I imagine talking to his two friends will be just as useful."

"He's probably on his phone now, warning them," Zach said.

They climbed into the truck.

Lani sighed. "We might as well head back to the rez. The other two guys won't be home."

"What about hitting up some of Mark's customers?" Zach suggested.

"It's not like they'll just walk into the station and confess to buying drugs from Mark," Lani said.

"No, but you have to have arrested some of them for public intoxication or something," Zach suggested.

"Let's head back to the station where I can ask my chief who is most likely to open up about his drug dealing with Mark."

Zach nodded and helped her up into the truck, his hand resting on her leg for a little longer than necessary.

When she settled into her seat, she looked over at Zach as he slid behind the steering wheel. "Thanks for coming along on this ride with me."

"I don't feel very useful."

"You are. I know that I don't have to watch my

156

back when you're around. Especially now that I've been warned that I'm next on the killer's list."

"Seems he jumped the gun with Mark."

"Maybe he hadn't intended to kill Mark. He didn't stab Mark like he stabbed Tyler and Ben."

"Yeah, and he tried to make it appear as if Mark committed suicide."

Lani shook her head slowly. "To me, it almost appears that Mark's attack was committed by a different person from the one who committed the first two murders." As soon as she said the words out loud, the idea made more sense.

"Holy hell," she murmured. "We have two killers loose on the reservation."

CHAPTER 10

Zach chewed on Lani's words, not feeling any better about the situation with every passing minute. When they arrived at the station, he held back. "You go on in. I need to touch base with my boss. He might have some insight or maybe provide some help looking into the backgrounds of different people."

"I'd like to know more about Ben and Mark Wolf Paw, as well as Russell Bledsoe."

Zach nodded. "I'll see what he can do. I know his computer guy has some special skills when performing background checks."

"Good." Lani slipped out of the seat onto the ground. "I'll talk with my boss and see if he's familiar with any other drug busts and who was involved. Some of those people might have been Mark's customers. They might have taken exception to Mark losing all their product."

"Giving them a motive to kill," Zach finished.

She nodded. "Exactly."

"I'll see you inside, after I talk with Hank."

Lani gave him a brief smile and entered the station.

Zach scrolled through his cellphone contacts, found Hank's number and placed the call.

The head of the Brotherhood Protectors answered on the first ring. "Hey, Zach, how's it going?"

"Not great," Zach responded.

"I got that feeling when I saw your call come through," Hank said. "I haven't heard from you since you left here, but I understand there was another murder last night."

"There was," Zach said. "The local drug dealer. The body was dumped in the lake, along with his motorcycle. We think the killer tried to make it look like a suicide." He explained his visit to the coroner and the evidence of a struggle visible on the body.

"The killer's body count is up to three," Hank said. "Need some help?"

"Maybe." Zach went on to explain Lani's theory that the first two murders were different than the third. "We might have more than one killer. And someone trashed Lani's house and left a message. The word 'Next'."

Hank whistled. "Look, I can send more help. All you have to do is say the word."

"Right now, I'm living on the reservation with Lani as her fiancé. No one is questioning my right to be here. The elders aren't that keen on outsiders poking their noses into reservation business. I get a free ride since I'm with Lani. The best you could do for me now is run some background checks on the following people: Russell Bledsoe, Mark Wolf Paw, Ben Wolf Paw, Tyler Lightfoot, Mattie Lightfoot and..." he hesitated, then added, "Raymond Swiftwater."

"I'll get Swede right on it," Hank promised. "And, Zach, don't hesitate to call if there's anything else you need. I have access to aircraft that could get me and half a dozen of my guys to you in less than an hour."

"That's good to know." Zach smiled into the phone. "I'll let you know if I need that kind of assistance." He liked that Hank was willing to throw everything he could at a situation, no matter the cost. How often had he gone into battle without backup? Too many times, he hadn't even had the full buy-in from his commanding officers.

Hank Patterson was everything he'd heard about and more. He cared about his people and was there if they needed him.

Zach rang off and entered the police station.

Lani was deep in conversation with the chief. She motioned him over and continued. "I'm telling you, Mark's murder was different. Either it was another killer, or the killer got sloppy."

"Could it be he killed Mark for different reasons?" the chief suggested. "Mark was the reservation drug dealer."

"Which leads to my next question…" Lani drew in a deep breath. "Who were his clients?"

"It might be easier to ask who wasn't one of his clients." The chief ran a hand through his hair. "We've picked up a number of people who've been strung out on drugs. We suspect they were using some of the illegal substances we found in Mark's trailer.

"Why would Mark have all that stuff out on his kitchen table?" Zach asked.

"I'm betting he was getting ready to move it," Black Knife said. "Or he'd just moved it to the trailer after his brother's death, and he was just starting to pack it away when Running Bear showed up."

"He had to know someone would be out to the trailer to ask him questions about his brother's death." Lani shook her head. "It doesn't make sense."

"Maybe his former hiding place was compromised, and he had to move it in a hurry," the chief said. "We might never know, since Mark can't answer any of our questions. The FBI agent went back to Great Falls. He'll be back after he does some research on his database back at his office. In the meantime, I have three dead Blackfeet and a group of elders breathing down my neck."

"Would it help for me to go back out to the lake and look again for evidence?" Lani asked.

"We combed that area," the chief said. "Whoever dumped Mark was good at covering his tracks."

"He had to have missed something," Lani said.

Black Knife snorted. "Yeah, like he missed at the Lightfoot home or Ben's place."

"Oh, and speaking of elders," Lani said. "You'll be happy to know Swiftwater is conducting his own investigation."

The chief swore. "What's he up to now?"

"He was at the coroner's office when we got there. He stayed while the coroner gave us his preliminary findings."

"Great, just what we need...an elder mucking up our investigation. I never did like Swiftwater. Why he's one of the elders, I'll never know." The chief scratched his chin. "He can't stay out of our business, and yet he can't keep his son employed. Not the best qualifications for an elder, if you ask me."

"What's wrong with his son?" Zach asked.

"He didn't show up for work this morning." The sheriff's brow furrowed. "I had coffee with his boss. He was complaining about the fact Alan hadn't come to work, nor had he bothered to call to explain why."

Lani recalled Swiftwater getting the call about his son missing work while he was at the coroner's office. "Do you think something happened to his son? Maybe the killer targeted him as well."

The chief shook his head. "That boy has never had to live up to his responsibilities. His daddy keeps bailing him out whenever he fails to meet expectations. His job at the feed store...?" Black Knife jerked his head. "Ray got him that job by putting a little pressure on the owner. And what does the owner get in return? A deadbeat employee. I'd fire his ass. But he can't, or Daddy Swiftwater will make his life miserable."

"Sounds like a winner," Lani said

"Granted, the kid has been sick lately, but no one knows whether it's real or due to substance abuse." The chief shrugged. "Either way, the least he could do is call in to his employer. Not showing up is rude and inconsiderate. Any employer would be within his rights to fire him. He'll be lucky to get another job anywhere near here without a decent reference."

Lani frowned, her thoughts going to the bar and her run-in with Alan Swiftwater. "Was Alan Swiftwater one of Mark's clients?"

The chief tilted his head considering her question. "If Alan is doing drugs, he could well have been."

Zach met her gaze. "He was at the bar when Mark came in."

Lani nodded. "He blocked my attempt to go after Mark."

"He was there to buy product from Mark," Zach concluded.

"Mark didn't have anything to sell, unless he had another stash outside his home," the chief said.

"Who knows what a man desperate for his next fix will do?" Lani said.

"He might have been angry when his dealer didn't come through for him," Zach said.

Lani drew a sharp breath. "Angry enough to beat him to death?"

The chief's brow formed a V on his forehead. "It's worth bringing Alan in for questioning. Since he didn't show up for work, we'll have to get creative about looking for him."

"We should start by going to his house," Lani said. "He lives with his father."

"If he were at his house, his boss would have gotten hold of his mother," the chief said. "She would have said something about him being there or not."

"Unless he's hiding out in his room and not answering his mother's calls," Lani said. "I'll swing by. Then I'll make a pass through town, looking for his red Mustang. It ought to be easy to spot."

"If he's in town at all. If he killed Mark Wolf Paw, he might be miles away by now," Zach said. "He could have crossed the border into Canada."

"Great." The chief planted his fists on his hips. "We could be dealing with a fugitive who has gone international. It'll take time to wade through the red tape of extradition."

"We can't worry about that now," Lani said. "First, we have to make certain Alan hasn't left the county, much less the country."

"Right," the chief said. "I'll put out an all-points bulletin on him. If anyone sees him, they're to proceed with caution and bring him back for questioning. We don't have any evidence that he was responsible for Mark's murder. We won't be able to hold him long."

"I still don't think the same man who killed Tyler and Ben killed Mark." She rubbed her arms. "It doesn't feel the same. It didn't fit the M.O. While we're chasing Alan Swiftwater, who may or may not have killed a drug dealer, the other killer is laughing at us and eyeing his next victim." She jabbed a thumb against her chest. "Me. He said I was next. Not Mark Wolf Paw."

"Good point," the chief said. "You should stay home and arm yourself. I'll get one of the other officers on duty to bring Alan in."

"I don't want to sit at home and wait for the killer to come to me," Lani said. "I just want to remind you that he's still out there. We have to keep open minds and eyes while we're out looking for Alan Swiftwater."

"Will do, Running Bear. Now, get your ass out there and find our killers," he said, pointing at the door. "I'll be out there doing the same. You got your radio?"

Lani patted her jacket pocket. "Got it."

"Good. Call me if you find them. Or if you get into any trouble. I'm going to check out the Swiftwater residence on the off-chance Alan's hiding there."

"We'll head out to the lake and look for anything you might have missed."

"I guess it doesn't hurt to have another pair of eyes on a crime scene," the chief said. "Be careful."

"Yes, sir." She popped a salute and turned to leave the building.

Zach chuckled when they reached his truck. "I thought for a moment the chief was going to pull you off the case again."

"He can't," Lani said and climbed into the passenger seat of the truck. "We're too shorthanded, and he needs all the people he can get looking for our killers."

"I would prefer to go back to your house and wait for the killer to show up. At least then, we'd have a defensible position."

"Yeah, but we don't know how long he'll take to make his move. I can't sit that long. I'd have to save him the bullet and shoot myself." She winked down at him as he closed the passenger door for her.

Lani's gaze followed him around the front of the truck, admiring the way he held himself. The man might be out of the military, but he hadn't lost an ounce of his military bearing. He held his broad shoulders back and squared. His torso narrowed to a slender waist and hips. The man walked with all the confidence of someone in charge of his own body and mind.

Damn, he was good looking. She'd much rather go back to her house and make love to him on the sleeping bag until the next day dawned, or longer. That just couldn't happen. Not with a killer on the loose and gunning for her. They'd taken chances the night before by making love and not paying attention to their surroundings. Sure, Zach had fixed the door frame and locked the door securely.

Still, the killer could have tossed a Molotov cocktail through the window and set the place on fire, burning them to crisps inside. Of course, he hadn't, and they'd explored each other's bodies thoroughly more than once.

The idea of repeating that exploration was so tempting, Lani almost threw her hands in the air and agreed to the chief's recommendation that she go back to her house and wait for the attack. At least then, she'd be alone with Zach. They might pick up where they'd left off and make love again. She stopped short of telling him to stop at the grocery store for more condoms. She didn't want to miss out on anything that might happen between them when they finally did retire to her house.

Before she could open her mouth to ask, they'd passed the grocery store and headed north toward the edge of town, moving slowly through the buildings. She focused on finding Alan's red Mustang. "If he was Mark's killer, and he thought he'd gotten away with passing it off as suicide, why would he hide? If I thought I'd gotten away with murder, I'd be out in the open."

"Remember, the M.E. said Mark got a piece of his killer. He scratched him." Zach slowed at a corner and looked left then right. "He might be hiding until the scratch heals."

"That could take days."

"Yeah, but how else would he explain it? And if his skin is as dark as yours, even after it heals—"

"It'll leave a pink or white mark for a lot longer." She nodded. "He'll have to hide for a while. Which is a good reason to avoid working in a public place. And he wouldn't be making any money, so he can't afford to go very far. He'll stay someplace where no one else goes." She looked across the console to Zach.

He nodded. "The abandoned warehouse." Zach goosed the accelerator, sending the truck shooting forward to the edge of town. Slowing slightly, he took the corner at the road leading out to the derelict building surrounded by chain link fence.

Lani leaned forward, her pulse racing, her hands clenched into fists. Excitement made her eyes shine and her cheeks darken.

Zach prayed they were on the right track. They had to be. He wasn't familiar with the area. He didn't know another place to look. Then he remembered Alan leaving the bar, shaking a cigarette out of a pack. A green and white pack. Just like the crumpled one Lani found in the warehouse. Swiftwater had used the site before. Surely, he'd use it again.

As they approached the abandoned warehouse, Zach slowed to a stop, two blocks before they reached the fence.

Lani's brow dipped, and she shot a quick glance toward him. "Why are you stopping here?"

"We're better off going the rest of the way on foot. If he's in there, we don't want him to hear the sound of my truck's engine. He might make a run for it."

Lani nodded. "You're right. We need to sneak up on him. If we see his car, we need to do something to disable it so he can't get away as easily as Mark did." She got out of the truck and started toward the old building.

Zach caught up with her and snagged her arm. "One thing."

"Yeah?" she asked her gaze on the building ahead of them.

"I go in first."

She turned back to him, her brow furrowing. "I'm the cop. You're—"

"Going in first. He wants to kill you. Not me."

"But he might kill you to get to me." She shook her head. "I can't let you go in first. This is my responsibility."

"If I have to handcuff you to the fence, I will. I'm going in first." His jaw set in a firm line. He wasn't going to let her go a step further until she agreed to his terms.

Lani looked from him to the building and back. "Okay. But I'm coming in right behind you." She punched his arm lightly. "Don't go and get yourself shot." Lani lifted up on her toes and pressed her lips to his in a brief kiss. "I kind of like having you around. Alive."

Zach wrapped his arms around her and kissed her thoroughly. "The feeling is mutual. I think we have chemistry, and I don't want to lose that anytime soon." He set her back on her feet. "Don't get yourself killed."

She stared up at him for a long moment. "You mean that?"

He locked his gaze with hers. "Every word. I've been thinking about you since Afghanistan. If you hadn't called me when you did, I was going to look you up."

Her face split in a grin. "Let's get this over with. I want to explore the possibilities with you more. When we're not hunting a killer."

"Deal." He led the way to the gap in the fence and went through first. He waited for her to follow, and then hurried toward the building, ducking into the shadows on the eastern side. As he rounded the corner of the building, Zach spotted the bumper of the red Mustang, parked behind a stack of pallets. He waited for Lani to catch up to him then pointed to the car.

She nodded. "Disable it," she whispered.

He nodded and headed for the car first, moving in the shadows until he reached the stack of pallets.

Zach stopped and listened for sounds of movement from the other side of the stack. Nothing indicated the car was occupied. He inched his way around the pallets and peered into the back window of the sports car.

It appeared to be empty.

Lani slipped up beside him. "Look at the trunk," she said.

Deep scratches marred the previously pristine paint job. It was as if something heavy and metal had been dragged across the paint. Maybe a dirt bike being shoved into the trunk?

Zach slipped up beside the vehicle. On the back seat lay a tire iron. The murder weapon?

The front driver's window was down, and the key was in the ignition.

Zach reached in, plucked the key out and slid it into his pocket.

Then he moved past the old car, heading for the door on the side of the building where they'd exited the last time they'd been there.

Lani kept up with him, moving silently, placing her feet carefully so as not to make a sound.

When he reached the door, he knew that if Alan

was inside, he'd hear the door opening. Their cover would be blown, and they'd have to move fast to catch him. Based on the location of his car, he had to have used this door to enter the building.

The last time he'd tried that door, it had been locked from the inside. Lani had unlocked it. If it was locked this time, they'd have to retrace their steps and swing around to the other side of the structure and enter through the missing panel.

Zach drew in a deep breath and held it. Then he gripped the handle and slowly turned it.

The knob turned, and the door opened.

Zach stood to the side, out of range, and let the door float open.

He leaned close to Lani and whispered in her ear. "Give me a second before you follow."

She nodded, her gun in her hand, her knees bent, and her stance ready.

Zach held his pistol in front of him as he slipped around the edge of the door and into the building. Immediately, he ducked to the side, out of the wedge of light shining on the floor.

He moved deeper, hunching low, his ears straining to hear even the slightest sound. A noise behind him made him glance back.

Lani had ducked through the door and now clung to a shadow close by. She was inside, following him. A chill slithered down the back of Zach's neck. He prayed she wasn't following him into danger. He had vowed to protect her, not get her deeper into trouble. Lani would be the first to jump in feet first. She had a duty to protect the people of her tribe, and she wouldn't quit until she found the killer or killers.

Zach faced forward, allowing his eyesight to adjust to the darkness. He searched shadows for movement. Taking a step forward, he felt the boards beneath him give, the wood crackling and creaking. Splinters of wood snapped. He didn't linger in one spot, afraid that if he did, the whole floor would give way, and he'd plunge to the basement level below.

Behind him, he heard the snap and crackle of tired boards, groaning beneath the weight of one slender woman. He wished he had a flashlight to illuminate the vast room to help him find the man they were looking for. But a flashlight would make him a target, giving a shooter something to aim for. He had to go with the faint glow from the open door on the side of the building. The deeper he moved into the building, the less light he had to work with. Soon, he couldn't see the hand in front of his face.

The key in his pocket reminded him that he had Alan's means of escape.

"Alan," Lani's voice echoed in the vast blackness. "We know you're here. We just want to talk to you."

Silence reigned.

"You're not going to get away," she said. "We have the keys to your car. The only way you're getting out of here is on foot." She paused.

Zach listened for a voice, the sound of movement, anything.

Nothing.

Lani continued. "I was a star runner on my track team in high school," she said. "And I always aced the run on my fitness test in the Army. You won't get far. And even if you get away from me, you won't get away from my fiancé."

Still, no response.

Zach drew in a deep breath and added his plea. "Alan, we know what you did to Mark. He didn't commit suicide. He fought hard to survive. And he has the DNA beneath his fingernails to prove who hurt him. You might as well save some time and turn yourself in."

The creak of a floorboard sounded ahead of Zach. He hurried toward the sound, intent on catching Alan before he ducked out an exit they had yet to discover.

Zach took another step. The floor beneath him suddenly gave way, a gaping maw opening up to swallow him. He fell through the jagged-edged boards and rotted timbers. He didn't stop until he crumpled to the solid concrete floor of the basement below. For a moment, he lay gasping for air, the breath having been knocked from his lungs when he hit bottom.

"Zach!" Lani cried out. "Zach! Where are you? Are you all right? Please, tell me you're all right."

Zach lay on his back staring upward, the only light coming from above through the hole in the floor he'd just fallen through. The glow was barely a lighter gray in the pitch blackness.

When he could fill his lungs again, he called out, "Go back, Lani. The floor isn't safe. Go back."

"Not without you," she said. "Where are you?"

"In the basement. I fell through the floor." He pushed to a sitting position, testing his muscles and bones. So far, nothing felt broken. Running his hands over his legs, he felt warm wetness on his right thigh. His fingers encountered a tear in his jeans and the flesh beneath stung when he touched it. One of the boards must have ripped a hole in his thigh. It didn't feel that deep. Thankfully, he wouldn't bleed out. But he was stuck in the dark, and he had to find his way out soon. Lani was alone above him. And she was next on the killer's agenda.

"Zach? Talk to me," she said. "Are you okay?"

"I'm okay. But I need you to get out of here. Now."

"I'm not leaving you."

"You have to. You're not safe on your own."

"I'm with you."

"Not when you're up there, and I'm down here." He pushed to his feet and winced at the pain shooting through his thigh. "You have to get out of here."

"I'm turning on a phone's flashlight," she said.

"No, Lani. You'll only make yourself a target."

"I can't help you, if I can't see you," she argued. "I'm following your voice."

"Don't," he cried out.

At that moment, the boards above snapped, and the warehouse floor caved in, bringing Lani down with a resounding thud.

"Lani?" he called out, feeling his way across the floor to where he hoped to find her.

A moan echoed against the walls around him.

"Lani, sweetheart, talk to me," he begged.

CHAPTER 11

"I'm okay," Lani said, though every bone in her body had been jolted hard in the fall, especially her tailbone.

"Can you move?" Zach asked.

She couldn't see him, only hear him, as he shuffled through the debris, his voice moving steadily toward her.

Lani pulled her cellphone from her jacket pocket and tried to turn on the flashlight app. She slid her finger across the screen, feeling the sharp lines of a huge crack. "Damn," she said. "It's broken."

"Dear, sweet Jesus, Lani," he said. "What's broken, babe? Does it hurt bad?"

She laughed. "No, no. I'm not in pain, except my sore tailbone," she said. "My cellphone is broken. I can't switch on the light."

"Oh, Lani, baby," Zach said. "You're going to be the death of me."

"That's where you're wrong," a voice said from above. A beam of light shined down on them, moving from Zach to where Lani lay among the rubble of the broken floor. "You shouldn't have come. You should have let Mark's death be what it was...suicide. Because he might as well have committed suicide when he let all his drugs get confiscated by the police. The jerk was so strung out on them, he didn't even try to take them with him. He ran, wasting everything. All he had left was a tiny baggy not even half full." Alan paused. "A tiny baggy. I paid for a lot more than that, yet he wasn't willing to give me even that pathetic amount."

"So, you took it from him using force," Zach said. "Isn't that right?"

"I had no choice," Alan said, his voice shaking. "I had no choice. I couldn't go another day without it."

"So, you killed him," Lani prompted.

"It doesn't matter," Alan said. "Everything is going to hell, and you're going with me." He set the flashlight on the ground, the beam shining at his feet. He leaned over and hefted a large can in his arms. "It's over. It's all over," he said, his voice breaking on a sob. Tipping the can, he poured liquid onto the floorboards above them.

Some of it splashed down on the concrete near

Lani. An acrid scent filled her nostrils and made her blood run cold.

Gasoline.

Lani pushed to her feet. "Alan, you don't want to do this."

"Yes. I do," he said. "I can't go to jail. They won't give me what I need. They can't fix what's broken, and they can't save the dying. I won't be here to watch it happen. I won't care."

"Alan, you're not making sense. Help us out of here. Let us get you the help you need. Killing us won't make things better. I promise you," Lani said.

"Maybe not, but if I die with you, they will blame me for all five deaths. No one will look further. No one will learn the truth."

"The truth about what?" Zach asked. "That you didn't kill Tyler or Ben?"

"Alan, we know you didn't kill Tyler and Ben," Lani said.

"You'll take that knowledge to the grave, along with me," Alan said. Sloshing gasoline over the floor above, he moved away from the gap in the floor.

Zach flicked on the flashlight in his phone. "Come on, we have to find a way out of here. Now." He took Lani's hand and helped her pick her way through the boards and trash on the basement floor, alternating between shining the light at their feet and pointing it at the walls.

"There has to be a staircase around here somewhere." Zach turned in a three-hundred-sixty-degree circle, shining the little phone flashlight around the huge expanse of basement beneath the warehouse. When the light fell on stairs leading up to the next level, he stopped. "Bingo." Gripping Lani's elbow in his hand, he hustled her toward the stairs.

"We might only have seconds before Alan lights a match and sets our world on fire. If we don't get out of here before that happens, we'll be trapped in the basement as the rest of the warehouse burns down around us," Lani said.

"You're not dying on my watch," Zach muttered, increasing their speed until they were running.

"Who said I was dying?" Lani reached the stairs first and climbed to the top, only to find a door blocking their exit. She pulled on the handle, giving it every bit of strength she could muster. It didn't budge.

"Move." Zach pushed past her, braced his foot on the wall beside the door, grabbed the handle and yanked hard. The door shook but didn't open.

"Again," Lani yelled, the scent of gasoline filling the air, making her gag.

Zach braced his foot again and pulled with all his might.

The door slammed open, nearly sending Zach flying down the steps.

Holding onto the doorknob, he regained his

balance and held the door wide, allowing Lani to go through first.

"Get outside as quickly as possible," he said and pushed her through the door. He followed right behind her, still shining the phone's light over her shoulder at what lay in front of Lani, so she didn't step on any more rotten boards.

As they neared the door they'd come through, Lani realized it was closed. They'd specifically left it open when they'd come through minutes before. She hurried forward and tried the handle. It didn't work. She twisted the locking mechanism, only to find it had been broken. The metal door had been jammed and locked permanently.

"Let me try," Zach said.

Lani moved out of the way.

Zach hit the door with his shoulder. The door didn't budge.

He hit it again and bounced back. Rubbing his shoulder, he drew in a deep breath and would have slammed into the door again, but Lani laid a hand on his arm.

"Don't," she said. "Alan jammed the lock. It's not going to open." She turned toward the interior of the warehouse. "We have to find another way out."

"There is no other way out," Alan shouted from across the floor.

Lani and Zach turned toward the sound.

Alan struck a match, held it up for a second,

lighting his face in an eerie glow. Then he tossed it into the warehouse through the gap in the exterior siding. Flames erupted on the gasoline-soaked wooden floor, shooting toward Lani and Zach.

Her heart stopped as Lani watched the flames racing toward her, lighting the interior of the old building.

Zach gripped her arm. "Move!" he shouted and dragged her away from the oncoming flames to a place on the floor where the wood was dull and dry.

Flames grew around them, consuming the gasoline Alan had sloshed sporadically throughout the structure.

"We have to make our way to the other side through the areas that aren't soaked in gasoline," Zach said. "And fast. It won't be long before the boards catch fire."

Lani nodded and followed him through the maze of flames, ducking low to avoid the rising smoke.

Between the fire and the rotten floor, they made painfully slow progress. Lani pulled her shirt collar up over her nose and picked her way over the dangerously unstable floor, praying they made it to the gap in the wall before the fire took root in the dry wood flooring and consumed it like tinder.

She coughed and sucked more smoke into her lungs, causing her to cough uncontrollably.

Zach grabbed her hand and dragged her through the smoke and flames.

At one point, he stepped on a board that cracked and splintered. He would have fallen through had Lani not jerked him back in time.

He changed direction and kept moving, pulling her along until they were within ten yards of the opening. Alan Swiftwater stood in the gap, a gun in his hand. "No way. You can't leave. I won't let you. They have to believe it was me all along."

"That you killed Mark?" Zach called out. "They'll know…" he coughed, "soon enough, when the DNA under his fingernails is analyzed." Covering his mouth again, he continued forward despite the gun pointed at his chest. "Don't add to the murder count, Alan. You don't want to kill us. They'll put you away for life."

"You don't understand. My life doesn't matter. I'm already dead. Everything and everyone I ever cared about is dead or dying."

Lani dropped the hand holding her shirt up over her mouth. Smoke stung her eyes and lungs. "What are you talking about?" She coughed, desperate to breathe fresh, clean air. "You have your father. He cares."

Alan shook his head. "No. He's dying. Can't you see?"

"No, Alan. I can't see," Lani said, blinking to help her see the man through the smoke. "What do you mean your father is dying?" Her lungs burned with each breath she took. If they didn't get out soon, the smoke would kill them before the flames could.

"If you continue your investigation," Alan said. "then everyone will know. He'll die in disgrace. I won't let that happen."

"Enough!" A deep voice shouted.

Another man stepped into the gap in the wall. A man of equal height to Alan but with broader shoulders and a more commanding presence.

Raymond Swiftwater glared at his son. "How dare you?"

"I couldn't let them take you away," his son said. "They don't know what I do."

"Shut up. You have no right to fight my battles. You can't. This is mine, and only mine to fight." He shook his head. "You fool. You would have had it all. My business, my money, my life after my death. Yet, you chose to throw it all away on drugs, and then murder." Raymond shook his head. "Why?"

"I wouldn't have had it all. I wouldn't have had you. And I couldn't survive without the drugs. I mean, look at me." He held out his gun, his hand shaking uncontrollably. "I killed a man because he couldn't give me what I needed."

"You shouldn't have done it," Raymond said.

Alan glared at his father. "*I* shouldn't have done it? What about *you*? Why Tyler and Ben? What did they ever do to you?"

"They had what I didn't, damn it," Raymond ground out.

"And what's that?" his son demanded. "A long life ahead of them?"

"Yes!" Raymond shouted.

Zach knelt on the wooden floor of the warehouse and drew his gun from his holster.

Shocked at Raymond's revelation, Lani dropped to her knees searching for better air to breathe, her hand going to her weapon as well.

"We have to get out of here," he said softly. "I'll distract them. You go. Slip up to the wall and wait for my signal. Then make a break for it."

She shook her head. "I won't leave without you."

"Just do it," he urged. "I'll get out after you're safe."

"No."

He cupped her face in his hands and kissed her lips in a brief but tender kiss. "I think I'm falling for you, Lani Running Bear. Live, so that I can find out if what I'm feeling is love." He nodded his head toward the gap and the two men blocking their escape. "Now, go."

"But—"

"Go!" Zach pushed to his feet and staggered to the right, away from Lani, but in the general direction of the Swiftwater men.

Lani darted in the other direction, moving toward the exterior wall and the shadows that would hide her until she could reach the gap. Her heart hammered against her ribs, and her lungs strained to pump oxygen into her system. She was dizzy, her chest burned and heart swelled with the knowledge that Zach might be falling in love with her. Living was the only option. For both of them.

When she arrived at the wall, she crept along the metal siding until she was within a couple yards of Alan and Raymond Swiftwater. She glanced toward the spot where she'd last seen the man she was quickly coming to love and gasped.

Zach rose out of a wall of flame, his arms extended like a phoenix rising from the ashes. He was bold, larger than life and magnificent. "Let us go free...or kill us now!" His announcement was then followed by coughing.

The two men stopped arguing and stared at Zach.

Alan raised his gun and aimed at Zach.

No!

While the Swiftwaters' attention was on Zach, Lani charged toward Alan.

The pop of gunfire sounded. One shot, then another.

Before she reached the younger Swiftwater, he slumped to the ground and lay still.

Lani stumbled and fell to her knees. She scrambled around to face the inferno and the position where Zach had made his stand. Who had fired the shots? Where was Zach?

Her gaze swept the raging fire to no avail. If he was there, he was down.

Beside Lani, Alan lay on the ground, unmoving. Raymond stood with his gun to his jaw. He stared down at her. "He was my son. I only wanted to know he would be okay when I died." His lips firmed. "Now, it doesn't matter." He pulled the trigger.

At the same time, an earsplitting crack sounded, followed by a deafening rumble. The roof of the warehouse swayed, and then fell, crashing inward.

As her world imploded around her, Lani screamed and fell to the ground. A cloud of smoke and dust consumed her.

WHEN ZACH HAD RAISED his arms, he'd cupped his weapon in his palm. With the flames behind him, he'd banked on the fact he'd be nothing but a silhouette to the men standing in the door. They wouldn't see that he had his gun. Given the circumstances, he would be forced to use it. He had to make sure Lani wasn't hurt when she made her move.

As Alan pointed his gun, Zach knew he had to shoot first or die in the flames.

He didn't get the chance to pull the trigger first. Alan's gun went off at the moment Zach ducked, lowered his weapon and pulled the trigger.

He dove toward a black spot on the floor where the flames had already consumed the gasoline.

Rolling to his feet, he was running for the opening when the roof shimmied, groaned and came down. As smoke and dust exploded outward, Zach held his breath and focused on getting the hell out of the building before he was crushed beneath the debris.

He ran blind, the air too thick to see through, his lungs burning from smoke and dust. He prayed he was still heading in the right direction as he sprinted, running as far and fast as he could.

Zach didn't stop until he cleared the cloud of dust and smoke and witnessed blue sky overhead. Only then did he stop and drag in a breath of clean, fresh air. He blinked to clear the grit of smoke from his eyes and stared back at the billowing cloud rising up from what was left of the dilapidated warehouse. Nothing moved out of the cloud. No one moved.

Lani.

Taking a deep breath of smoke-free air, he ran back into the cloud. "Lani!" he shouted. "Lani!"

The roar of the flames and the rumble of struts and timbers crashing in drowned out his calls.

Smoke made his eyes burn and tears form, washing the grime from his eyes. "Lani!" he called out.

He found the side of the building and felt his way along the wall, trying and failing to find the woman who'd shown him what a beautiful place his Montana was. The woman who'd brought his heart to life and given him hope for the future. A future in the state he thought he'd left forever. A future that might include a strong, beautiful woman.

"Lani!" When he came to the gap in the wall, he dropped to his knees and felt his way along the ground, searching for life. Searching for her.

His fingers encountered a lump. A body. Zach waved a hand over it in an attempt to identify who it was. The smoke cleared enough, Zach could see the face beneath him, and he let out a cry of disappointment and relief.

It wasn't Lani.

Alan Swiftwater lay in a pool of his own blood, his eyes staring up into the dirty cloud.

Zach moved past him to another dark figure lying in the dirt.

Raymond Swiftwater. He couldn't tell by the man's face, as it had been blown away and was nothing more than a bloody mess. But he'd been the only other man out there. It was him. And he was dead.

Knowing the smoke would kill her if the Swiftwaters hadn't already, Zach pushed past the deceased men and almost cried when he found her body, lying in the dirt.

Scooping her up in his arms, he walked in the direction he hoped would take him away from the fire and smoke. Soon, the cloud thinned, and he stood beneath the clear, blue Montana sky, sucking clean air into his smoke-filled lungs.

He kept walking until he was certain the smoke wouldn't shift in his direction. Then he laid Lani on the ground, pulled his cellphone out of his pocket and dialed 911.

Even before the dispatcher answered his call, he could hear the sound of sirens wailing. In the next few minutes, fire trucks arrived, and emergency medical technicians gathered around them and took over.

While one paramedic slipped an oxygen mask over Lani's face, another handed one to Zach and commanded, "Breathe."

He brushed the man's offering aside. "Not until she does."

"She will. But you're no good to her, if you don't do the same." Again, he handed the mask to Zach.

Taking it, he placed it over his nose and mouth and breathed in the oxygen. When he dissolved into a fit of coughing, he flung the mask aside and dragged in more air, feeling as if he would suffocate behind the mask.

The paramedic lifted the mask back up to his face. "Keep breathing the oxygen. Though you're out of the smoke and fire, your lungs might be damaged. You need this." He tipped his head toward Lani. "She needs it."

Zach covered his nose and mouth again. "I'm riding with her to the hospital." It wasn't a question. He would go, whether they wanted him to or not.

Chief Black Knife arrived in his service vehicle and ran to where the emergency technicians were loading Lani into the back of an ambulance. "Is she okay?" he asked.

"I don't know." Zach shoved a hand through his sooty hair, more exhausted than he'd ever felt after a battle. "She's not dead."

But she could still die. Smoke inhalation could claim her even after they'd removed her from the fire.

"What happened?" the chief asked.

Between hacking coughs, Zach gave the chief a digest version of what had occurred.

"Swiftwater?" the older man shook his head. "No wonder he didn't want too many people digging into the murders. But his son?" He sighed. "I guess the apple didn't fall far from the tree."

The firefighters had tamped down the flames, and the smoke had begun to clear, exposing the two bodies lying near the building.

"I'd like to think I was the one who killed Alan Swiftwater," Zach said. "Based on the direction of his wound, I think his father did. Not from my lack of trying. I was inside the building facing him when I fired my weapon. He was aiming at me; however, his wound was in his side. I suspect his father shot him."

"They'll conduct an autopsy," the chief said. "I assume you'll be sticking around?"

Zach nodded and climbed into the ambulance with Lani. "Damn right, I will."

The door shut between him and the chief, and the ambulance raced toward Cut Bank, the reservation not having sufficient medical facilities to handle a severe case of smoke inhalation.

Zach sat beside the paramedic, holding Lani's hand, willing her to get well and be her usual, smart, strong and sassy self. If he hadn't known it before, he knew now that he loved this woman, and he wanted her to be all right, even if she didn't love him back.

CHAPTER 12

LANI WOKE the next day in the hospital. Her throat was sore, and her lungs felt like hell, but the sun shone through the window. She was alive.

"About time you woke up," a voice said.

She turned her head toward the door where a nurse in blue scrubs pushed a cart with a computer perched on top. "I'm Arianna, your nurse. I'm here to get your vital signs."

"How long?" Lani whispered, her words barely making it past her vocal cords.

"They brought you in yesterday afternoon. The doctor gave you a sedative to help you rest. You were fighting everyone when they tried to get you into that bed." She held out a thermometer. "Under your tongue, please."

Lani opened her mouth, allowing the nurse to

stick the thermometer under her tongue. She wanted to ask but was afraid of the answer.

Where was Zach?

"From what I understand, you're lucky to be alive. That fire on the reservation flared and burned into the night. They say there wasn't anything left but melted metal siding and a concrete basement when it finally burned itself out. Some people died." She shook her head as she wrapped the blood pressure cuff around her upper arm. "Yes, ma'am, you're lucky to be alive."

Tears welled in Lani's eyes. When the nurse plucked the thermometer from her lip, Lani mustered the courage to ask. "What about..." she croaked. Clearing her throat, she started over. "What about my...fiancé?" She held her breath, crossed her fingers and prayed.

The woman had her stethoscope in her ears, listening to Lani's heartbeat. When she looked up, she frowned. "Did you say something?"

"Yes," Lani gushed, letting go of the breath she'd been holding. "What about my fiancé, Zach Jones?"

Her words came out loud and clear.

"Did someone say my name?" a deep, raspy voice said from the door to her room. Zach entered the hospital room, carrying a huge bouquet of daisies in a clear glass vase and a small duffel bag. He dropped the duffel bag, plunked the vase on the rolling table, bent and pressed a kiss to her forehead. "Hey, beautiful."

Lani flung her arms around his neck and pulled him down in a hug so tight, he had no choice but to let her have her way with him. "Oh, Zach. Thank God. Thank God," she said. Tears flowed down her cheeks, making gray spots of residual soot on the white hospital sheets. "I thought you died in the fire. The roof, the smoke. How the hell did you get out?" She laughed and let him straighten, a smile permanently affixed to her face. "Oh, who cares? You're alive. That's all that matters."

She felt like hell, probably looked like it, but she couldn't stop grinning. "You're alive."

He nodded, a smile spreading across his face. "And so are you. For a while there, I thought it was touch and go." Zach lifted her hand and kissed the backs of her knuckles, his brow dipping low on his forehead. "With all that smoke and dust blanketing the building and the areas surrounding the ware-house, I didn't think I'd find you in time. I have to admit...it scared years off my life."

She brought his hand to her cheek. "You found me."

"Yes, I did. And you're going to be fine. The doctor said so. In fact, he's signed your discharge papers. I get to take you home." He reached for the bag he'd dropped on the floor and dropped it on the bed. "You'll find shampoo, a hairbrush, clothes and unmentionables in there. Enough to get you cleaned up and ready to go home."

"Really?"

The nurse winked. "Really. You can use the shower in the bathroom. I put clean towels in there this morning."

Lani threw back the sheets and swung her legs over the side of the bed. "I'll be ready in two shakes." She stood, swayed and would have fallen if Zach hadn't been there to catch her.

"Whoa, take a baby step at a time. You were on death's door a short time ago."

"I'm okay," she assured him. "I just got up too quickly." Lani squared her shoulders and met his gaze. "See? I'm okay."

"Maybe I should help you into the bathroom to make sure you don't pass out and drown," Zach said with a wicked grin.

"Do you want to get out of here, or stay a little longer?" she asked, her brow rising.

"Tough decision." He glanced toward the bathroom. "How big is that shower?"

"Seriously?" the nurse said, frowning. "Let the woman get cleaned up. This is a hospital, not a hotel."

Zach laughed out loud. "Go on, get your shower…alone."

Lani hesitated, chewing on her bottom lip.

He gave her a twisted grin. "Don't worry. I'll be here when you get out."

She walked toward the bathroom.

"Uh, Lani?" he said.

She turned to see him smiling. "What?"

"That gown opens in the back." He winked.

Heat burned her cheeks. She dove for the bathroom and slammed the door between them. He was right, the gown was open, and she wasn't wearing anything beneath it.

Lani yanked the gown off, turned on the water and didn't wait for it to warm before she stepped beneath the spray. She needed the cooling effect of the water to tamp down the fire raging at her core. Once she got back to her house, she'd roll out the sleeping bag and make love to him until neither one of them could stand. Then she'd make love to him again.

Using a significant amount of soap and shampoo, she scrubbed at the soot covering every inch of her body. When the gray water ran clear down the drain, she turned off the water, dried her body, brushed the tangles from her hair and rummaged through the bag of clothing.

She didn't recognize any of it.

"Um, Zach?" she called out.

"Yes, dear?" he answered as if he were standing on the other side of the door. "Are you all right?"

"I'm fine. Are you sure you grabbed the right bag? Not someone else's?"

"A friend of mine helped me pack it. Ray Swiftwater destroyed all of your clothing with spray paint. The items in your bag are new, donated by Hank Patterson's wife. She assured me they would fit. She had me check the sizes on your ruined clothes, so she'd know what to pack."

Lani lifted a sunny yellow cashmere sweater out of the bag and held up to her chest, looking at it against her skin in the mirror. The color complemented her coloring beautifully.

A white lacy bra and matching panties fit her perfectly. She pulled on the yellow sweater and a pair of cocoa-colored trousers and a pair of slim, black flats for her feet. "Could I hire Hank's wife to clothes shop for me again?" Lani said as she opened the door and stepped out.

Zach's smile faded, and his eyes rounded. "Wow."

"I know, right?" She turned around to give him a full perspective of the outfit. "She's amazing."

"*You're* amazing." He drew her into his arms and kissed her soundly on the lips before setting her at arm's length. "Ready?"

She laughed. "Yes. But I want to go shopping with Hank's wife again. Think she would take me?"

"You'll have to ask her. She's pretty busy between her job and their baby."

"What does she do?"

"Movies," Zach said. He gathered the plastic bag full of her sooty clothing and the duffel bag he'd brought with him containing the toiletries and clothes.

"Movies?" Lani asked, following him out the door of the hospital. "Have I seen her in anything?"

"Most likely."

"Patterson…" She shook her head. "I don't remember an actress with the last name of Patterson."

"She doesn't go by Patterson. She goes by McClain. Sadie McClain."

Lani stopped in the middle of the hallway. "*The* Sadie McClain?"

He looked back, frowning. "Yes, of course."

Lani squealed. "Sadie McClain picked out my clothes?" She looked down at the outfit and shook her head. "How can you be so nonchalant?"

Zach shrugged. "They're just clothes."

"Clothes picked out by Sadie McClain." Lani slipped her hand into his and hugged his arm. "That's the second-best thing to happen to me today."

"What was the first?" he asked, smiling down at her as they walked toward the exit.

She hugged his arm again, the smile slipping from her lips. "Waking up to find you alive."

Zach stopped in the middle of the hallway, dropped the bags and gathered her into his arms. "You were the best thing to happen to me in my entire lifetime." He crushed her lips in a kiss that curled her toes and left her breathless.

"Yowzah," a nurse murmured as she passed them. "You're making me jealous. My husband doesn't ever kiss me like that."

Zach retrieved the bags and hurried Lani out of the hospital. He filled her in on his conversation with the police chief and what they'd found in Alan and Raymond's vehicles. The tire iron in Alan's Mustang had hairs from Mark's scalp. Raymond had hidden the knife and baseball bat he'd used to kill Tyler and Ben under the mat in the back of his SUV. The police chief was certain they'd find enough DNA on both to be certain Raymond had killed them.

"And Hank's computer guy, Swede, hacked into Raymond's home computer and found emails and reports confirming Raymond had been diagnosed with pancreatic cancer." Zach shook his head. "The man was dying. He'd saved his suicide note, explaining his reasons for killing Tyler and Ben. They had everything going for them: they were well liked and set for a long, happy life, something Raymond wouldn't have. Apparently, he was jealous and angry and decided if he had to go, he was taking them with him."

Knowing who killed Tyler and Ben wouldn't bring them back, but Tyler's grandmother would have closure.

"I have a little surprise for you," Zach said as they drove through Browning and turned onto her street.

There were several cars parked against the curb

and a couple alongside hers in the driveway. But that wasn't what caught her attention. "My house!" she cried out. "The paint's gone."

"Not only is the red paint gone," Zach grinned, "the entire exterior and interior of the house has been repainted."

Lani shook her head. "How?"

"Did I tell you that I work for the Brotherhood Protectors?"

She nodded. "I know that."

"Well, when they heard what happened here, they piled into their vehicles and drove the five hours from Eagle Rock to Browning and worked all night and morning to paint and repair what was damaged. They even hauled off the broken furniture and trash to the dump."

Lani's eyes filled with tears.

Zach dropped down from the truck, hurried around to her side and helped her to the ground. "That's not all."

"What do you mean? Not all?" She laughed. "Isn't that enough?"

He shook his head. "They all pitched in," he said, guiding her up the steps to the front entrance. The door opened and a smiling Sadie McClain stood there, larger than life and as beautiful in person as she was on the big screen. "Welcome home, Lani."

Behind her were at least a dozen other people, male and female, holding cans of beer and glasses of wine. A man carrying a small child on his arm slipped a hand around Sadie. "Lani, I'm Hank Patterson. This is my wife, Sadie, and our baby, Emma. I hope you don't mind that a few of us made ourselves at home." He stepped back and let Lani walk into the room.

The place had been transformed from a disaster to a place that belonged on the cover of a home design magazine. A new sofa and easy chair stood in the living room on a bright, clean area rug. Beautiful artwork graced the freshly painted walls.

Broad-shouldered men filled the space with lovely women at their sides. A large German Shepherd leaned against one of the men's legs.

Zach leaned close. "The dog's name is Six. Don't worry, he won't bite."

Lani looked up at the man with the dog. "Can I pet him?"

The man nodded.

Lani, in a state of shock, held out her hand for the dog to sniff before she reached out to scratch behind his ear.

He nuzzled her hand, his tail thumping against the floor.

"Come see your bedroom," Sadie said. "If you don't like the furnishings, you can tell me. It won't hurt my feelings. It was all I could get delivered overnight."

Lani entered her bedroom, stunned at the

gorgeous wood furniture and the soft white comforter spread out over a brand-new mattress. "This is too much," she said. "I can never repay you for all you've done."

"No payment required," Hank said. "It was worth it to see Sadie in action, ordering all of this and getting the store owners to ship it overnight. Not only is the woman a phenomenal actor, she knows how to get people motivated."

Sadie blushed and took the baby from her husband's arms. "Don't let him kid you. Hank got all these men and women to paint the house inside and out in less than twelve hours. That's what I call amazing."

Lani walked back into the living room, her head spinning and her legs growing weaker.

"Sweetheart, you need to sit," Zach said. "You aren't yet fully recovered." He walked her to the sofa and insisted she sit.

"We would have left before you got here, but we had a few finishing touches to do to the exterior," Hank said.

"And we wanted to see your reaction," Sadie said with a smile. "But we're all heading back to Eagle Rock tonight. Emma sleeps best in her own bed. Although she did well camping out in her playpen overnight while we worked." Sadie kissed her baby's chubby cheek and hugged her close. "We have a long drive back, or we'd visit longer. If you're ever down around Eagle Rock, please come stay with us."

"Thank you," Lani said. "Thank you all for everything. I don't know what else to say." She stood again and walked with the men and women who'd given so much of their money and time to put her place back together so beautifully.

Hank and Sadie were the last two to say goodbye.

Hank turned to Zach. "Now that this case is closed, when can I expect you back in Eagle Rock?"

Lani shot a glance toward Zach, her eyes wide. She wasn't ready to lose him. She suspected she'd never be ready to lose this man she'd come to love the first time they'd met in Afghanistan.

Zach glanced down at her and smiled. "Sir, if it's all right with you, I'd like to base my work out of Browning. Now that I've found my roots, I want to stay and explore my heritage."

Hank's lips twisted. "Roots? Is that what they're calling it now?" He winked. "I wish you both all the happiness together." He hugged Lani. "I hope you feel better soon. The Blackfeet Law Enforcement team has a gem in you. If you ever decide it's not enough to keep you busy, I'd be happy to have you join my team of Brotherhood Protectors."

Lani's heart swelled at the compliment. "Thank you. I'll keep that in mind. Right now, I just want to do what I can for my people. I like to think they need me."

"Oh, they need you all right," Hank said.

Sadie leaned close with Emma and gave Lani a hug. "Remember, come visit. We love having guests. Especially, if they're like family."

"I suspect all your Brotherhood Protectors are like family," Lani said.

Sadie grinned. "They are. I love them all." She led the way to their truck, strapped Emma into her car seat and soon they were driving away, leaving Zach and Lani alone in her beautiful home.

"You need to sit. Having all those people here when you got home was too much."

"It was perfect," Lani said as she walked back into the house that twenty-four hours before looked like a war zone. "I don't deserve all this. It's too much."

"Everyone pitched in. They all wanted to help." Zach urged her to sit on the sofa, and he sat beside her. "Now that the murders have been solved and you're safe, you don't need me anymore. Say the word, and I'll leave."

She reached out and took his hand. "These past few days have made me realize something."

He lifted her hand to his lips and kissed her fingertips. "Yeah?"

"Yeah," she said. "It's made me realize what I've been missing in my life."

"Your own personal bodyguard?"

She chuckled. "That and more. You're like the mirror to my soul," she said softly. "I've never been one to get all soft and squishy, but you bring it out in me. I like having you around. All these years, I thought I was fine on my own. Independent, never needing anyone."

"And now?" he asked, kissing her knuckles and pulling her closer.

"Now, I know I need you. I need you like I need air to breathe."

He laughed. "And we've both been short of air."

She nodded. "When I woke up in the hospital, all I could think about was you. I had to know if you were okay. When you showed up, carrying that huge bouquet of flowers, I could breathe again." She leaned into him, pressing her cheek to his chest, listening to the beat of his heart that matched hers. "Is it crazy to think I could fall in love with you after such a short time?"

"If it is," he said, "call me crazy, too. I thought I'd lost you." He pulled her into the shelter of his arms and held her close and tight. "I've never felt so desperate and devastated when I thought you were gone. And when I found you…" He pressed his cheek to the top of her head. "My world became complete."

"Will it always be this good?" she asked.

"No. I'm sure there will be times when we don't even like each other."

"But we'll always love each other," Lani said. "And that's all that counts."

"Yes, ma'am." He kissed the top of her head and

stood. "With all the wonderful things they brought to your house, they tried to get rid of some things they thought you might not need anymore." Zach reached beneath a new end table and pulled out his neatly tied sleeping bag and held it up. "Do you want me to put it back behind the seat of my truck?"

Lani's lips curled and heat coiled at her core. She lifted her hand to Zach.

He took it and pulled her to her feet.

"You're not getting rid of that." She took it from him and hugged it to her chest. "We still have need of this."

"You have a perfectly fine bed now, complete with sheets and blankets.

"I do." She canted her head to one side. "But wouldn't it be even more comfortable if we had a sleeping bag on top of it? You know…so we can pretend we're camping out in a ravaged home, cele-brating the fact that a killer didn't succeed in getting to his next victim."

"I'm all for a little role playing." He scooped her up in arms, sleeping bag and all, and carried her to her new bed, where they made love in his old sleeping bag.

Life was good. The spirits smiled down on them, and Lani knew she'd found what she'd never known she was searching for.

She'd found love.

THE END

Thank you for reading Ranger Creed. The Brotherhood Protectors Series continues with Delta Force Rescue. Keep reading for the 1st Chapter.

INTERESTED IN MORE MILITARY romance stories? Subscribe to my newsletter and receive the Military Heroes Box Set

https://dl.bookfunnel.com/tug00n7mgd

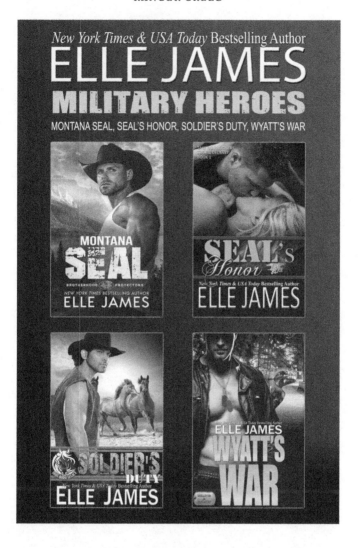

DELTA FORCE RESCUE

BROTHERHOOD PROTECTORS BOOK #15

New York Times & *USA Today*
Bestselling Author

ELLE JAMES

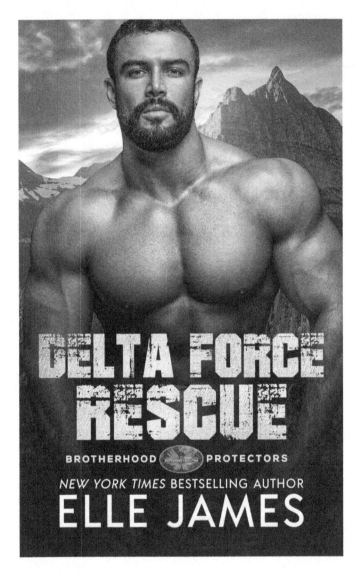

DELTA FORCE RESCUE

BROTHERHOOD PROTECTORS

NEW YORK TIMES BESTSELLING AUTHOR

ELLE JAMES

CHAPTER 1

BRIANA HAYES HITCHED up her leather satchel, resting the strap on her shoulder as she walked down the stairwell of the rundown apartment building. The day had been long and depressing. She'd already been to six different homes that day. Two of the parents of small children had threatened her. One child had to be removed and placed with a foster family after being burned repeatedly with a cigarette by the mother's live-in boyfriend. Some days, Briana hated her job as a Child Welfare Officer for the state of Illinois. Most days, she realized the importance of her work.

Her focus was the safety of children.

Thankfully, the last home had been one in which the mother seemed to be getting herself together for the love of her child. Because of drug abuse, she'd lost her baby girl to the state. After rehab treatment, she'd gotten a job, proved that she could support herself and the baby and regained custody. Briana prayed the woman didn't fall back into old habits. The child needed a functioning mother to raise her.

The sun had slid down below the tops of the surrounding buildings, casting the streets and alleys into shadow. A chill wind blew dark gray clouds over the sky. The scent of moisture in the air held a promise of rain. Soon.

Briana picked up her pace, hurrying past an alley toward the parking lot where she'd left her small non-descript, four-door sedan. A sobbing sound caught her attention and she slowed. She glanced into the dark alley, a shiver of apprehension running the length of her spine. This part of Chicago wasn't the safest to be in after sunset. Though she didn't want to hang around too long, she couldn't ignore the second sob.

"Hello?" she called out softly.

The sobbing grew more frequent, and a baby's cry added to the distress.

Despite concern for her own safety, Briana stepped into the alley. "Hey, what's wrong? Can I help?"

"No," a woman's voice whispered. "No one can." Though she spoke perfect English, her voice held a hint of a Spanish accent.

Briana squinted, trying to make out shapes in the

shadows. A figure sat hunkered over, back against the wall, holding a small bundle.

"Tell me what's troubling you. Maybe I can help." Briana edged nearer, looking past the hunched figure for a possible trap. When nothing else moved in the darkness, she squatted beside a slight woman, wearing a black sweater and with a hood covering her hair. She looked up at Briana, her eyes red-rimmed, tears making tracks of her mascara on her cheeks.

The baby in her arms whimpered.

"What's your name?" Briana asked.

"I can't." The woman's shoulders slumped.

"My name is Briana," she said. "I just want to know your name."

For a long moment, the young mother hesitated. Then in a whisper, she said, "Alejandra."

"That's a pretty name," Briana said, in the tone she used when she wanted to calm someone who was distraught. "And the baby?"

The woman smiled down at the infant in her arms. "Bella."

"She's beautiful." Briana couldn't leave them alone in the alley. "Do you need help getting home?"

She shook her head. "I can't go there."

"Has someone hurt you?" Briana asked, pulling her phone out of her pocket. "I can call the police. We can have him arrested."

"No!" The woman reached out and grabbed Briana's wrist.

Alarm race through Briana. Instinctively, she drew back.

The woman held tightly to Briana's wrist, balancing the baby in the curve of her other arm. "Don't call. I can't... He can't know where I am."

"If he's threatening you, you need to let the police know," Briana urged, prying the woman's hand free of her wrist. "They can issue a restraining order against him." When the woman shot a glance around Briana, Briana looked back, too. A couple walked past the end of the alley without pausing.

"Are you afraid to go home?" Briana asked.

"I have no home." The mother released Briana's arm and bent over her baby, sobbing. "He had it burned to the ground."

Briana gasped. "Then you *have* to go to the police."

She shook her head. "They can't stop him. He doesn't even live in this country."

"Then how...?"

"He has people," she said. "Everywhere."

Briana sank to her knees beside her. "Why is he doing this to you?"

The woman looked from the baby in her arms up to Briana. "He wants my baby. He won't stop until he has her."

Briana studied the woman and child as the first drops of rain fell. "You can't stay out here. You and the baby need shelter." She reached out her hand. "Come. You can stay at my apartment."

"No." Alejandra shrank against the wall, drawing the baby closer to her. "It's too dangerous for you."

"I'll take my chances," Briana reassured her.

"No. I won't do that to you. He will kill anyone who interferes with his attempt to take my daughter."

"Is he the father?" Briana asked.

Alejandra choked on a sob. "Yes. He is. But he's a very bad man."

"How so?"

"He is *El Chefe Diablo*," Alejandra whispered. "The head of the Tejas Cartel from El Salvador."

Though the word *cartel* sent a shiver of apprehension across Briana's skin, she couldn't ignore the woman and child's immediate needs. "I don't care if he's the head of the CIA or the Russian mafia, you and Bella can't stay out here in the rain. If not for yourself, you need to find real shelter for the baby." Again, she held out her hand. "Come with me. If you won't stay with me, we'll find a safe, anonymous place for you to stay."

Alejandra shook her head. "Anyone who helps me puts themselves in danger."

Briana firmed her jaw. "Again, I'll take my chances. And I know of a place where you won't be found. It's a privately run women's shelter where they don't take names and they don't ask too many questions."

Alejandra looked up, blinking as rain fell into her eyes. "I won't have to tell them who I am?"

"You won't," Briana assured her. She reached out again. "Come on. I'll take you there."

The woman clutched her baby closer. "You... you...aren't working for him, are you?"

"What?" Briana frowned. "No. Of course not. My job is to help children. Your baby needs protection from the rain. *You* need protection from the weather. If you don't come with me, I can't leave you. I'd have to stay here with you." She gave her a twisted smile. "Then we'd all be cold and wet."

"He always finds me. No matter where I go." Alejandra took Briana's hand and let her pull her to her feet. "I can't get away from him."

"We'll get you to the shelter. No one else has to know where you are. Just you, me and baby Bella."

"The people at the shelter?" she asked.

"Won't know who you are. You can tell them your name is Jane Smith."

Her eyebrows rose. "They won't require identification?"

"No. They've even helped immigrants who had nowhere else to turn." Briana slipped an arm around the woman and helped her to her car. "Come on. Get into my car. I can crank up the heater. You two will be warm in no time."

Briana helped Alejandra and the baby into the back seat of the car. "Hold on. I have a blanket I keep in my trunk." She rounded to the rear of the vehicle, popped the trunk lid and reached into the back where she kept a blanket, a teddy bear and bottles of water. She grabbed what she needed and closed the trunk.

Alejandra had buckled herself in and raised her shirt to allow the baby to breast feed.

Briana draped the blanket around the two, handed the woman the plastic bottle of water and laid the teddy bear beside her. "The shelter is about thirty minutes outside of Chicago. You might as well settle in for the ride."

Alejandra nodded and leaned her head back against the headrest. "Thank you." She closed her eyes, her arm firmly tucked around the baby nursing at her breast.

Briana climbed into the driver's seat, shifted into gear and drove out of Chicago to the shelter she knew that didn't require government assistance, therefore wasn't run with all the background checks or identification requirements. Alejandra and Bella would be safe there. Once she had them settled in, she could go home to her apartment, knowing the two were safe from harm and out of the weather, at least for the night.

Traffic was heavy getting out of the city. Eventually, she turned off the main highway onto a secondary highway, and then onto a rural Illinois county road.

A glance in her rearview mirror made Briana smile.

Alejandra, Bella lying in her arms, slept, her tired face at peace except for the frown tugging at her brow.

The wife or girlfriend of the leader of a drug cartel... Briana had run into women who had been on the run from drug dealers, mafia or gang members. Each had been terrified of being found, of their children being taken from them, or murdered. Their fears were founded in truth. Briana had witnessed the aftermath of a gang member's vengeance, and the memory still haunted her. She found it incomprehensible that a man could murder a woman and child out of sheer hatred.

The shelter was located at what had once been a dairy farm. The huge old barn, where the cows had come to be milked, had been cleaned out and converted into living quarters for women and their small children who needed a place to hide away from brutal and abusive relationships. The foundation was funded by a celebrity who preferred to remain anonymous. The rumor had it that the celebrity had once been a woman in need of assistance and a safe house to live in.

Manned by licensed psychologists, social workers and occupational specialists, the shelter was there to provide a place to live and to help the residents learn new skills and, ultimately, become independent and able to take care for themselves. They also had an attorney on retainer to assist the women in getting the restraining orders, separation agreements and divorces they needed in order to start new lives away from toxic situations.

When they arrived at the shelter, Briana parked at the rear entrance, where the people who ran it preferred potential residents to enter. Though they were out in the county, the fewer people who knew of the comings and goings, the better they were able to keep women hidden from their abusive significant others.

As soon as they drove beneath the overhang, a woman emerged from the entrance, a smile and frown of concern on her face. She started to open the passenger seat door but quickly changed to open the back door. "Hello, I'm Sandy. Welcome to Serenity Place."

Briana smiled as she climbed out of the vehicle and stood beside Sandy. "Hi, Sandy. This is…Jane and her daughter, Jill. They need a safe place to stay."

Sandy held out her hand. "You've come to the right place. We're very discreet here. Our primary concern is for the safety of our residents, both big and small."

Alejandra took her hand and let her pull her and the baby out of the car. "Thank you."

In the next few minutes, the woman had Alejandra and Bella assigned to a room with a full-

ELLE JAMES

sized bed, a crib and a package of disposable diapers. Once Alejandra had changed Bella's diaper, Sandy took them to a dining room where she helped Alejandra make a sandwich.

"Would you like one, too?" Sandy asked Briana.

She shook her head, though her stomach rumbled. "No, thank you. I need to get back to the city before it gets much later." Briana hugged Alejandra and slipped a business card into her hand. "If you need anything, call me."

The young woman's eyes filled with tears. "You've already done so much."

Briana gave her a gentle smile. "Nothing more than anyone with an ounce of compassion would have done. Take care of yourself and your little one." She brushed a finger beneath the baby's chin then turned to leave.

Sandy followed her to the exit. "We'll take very good care of them."

Briana turned to Sandy. "She's scared. From what she's told me, some very bad people are after her. The baby's father has some connections. If they find her, it won't be good for her or the people harboring her."

"We've dealt with similar situations." Sandy touched her arm. "We'll be on the lookout."

"Thank you, Sandy," Briana said. "You have my number. Call me if you need anything or have any concerns."

She nodded. "Be careful driving back into the

city."

Briana climbed into her car and headed for Chicago. All along the way, she thought about Alejandra and her baby. The desperation in the woman's eyes had struck a chord in Briana's heart. She'd seen that look before in the faces of young mothers she'd visited. Too often, they stayed in bad situations, thinking they had no other alternative. Alejandra had taken the step to get away from the man who'd threatened her and her child. It took a lot of courage to leave an abusive man. The least she deserved was a safe place to hide until she could get back on her feet, maybe change her identity and start a new life somewhere else.

Back at her apartment, Briana climbed the stairs to the second floor and let herself in.

"That you?" her roommate, Sheila Masters, called out from the kitchen.

"It's me," Briana answered as she dropped her keys on the table in the entryway.

"You're late getting home. Did you have a hot date?" Sheila stepped out of the kitchen and handed Briana a glass of wine.

"You're a godsend," Briana said, accepting the offering with a heavy sigh. "I need this and a long soak in a hot tub."

"Go for it. I'll be out here watching some television. I had a busy day at the office. I had to train the new hire." She carried her own wine glass toward the living room, talking as she went. "I don't know why I always get stuck training the new folks."

"Because you have the most patience of anyone in that office. Who else could do it?"

Sheila turned, her lips pinched together. "You're right. Sherry is short-tempered, Lana is too into Lana and Trent is too busy to train anyone himself."

"Which leaves you." Briana touched her friend's arm. "That's why I love you so much. You're the best friend a girl can have. And you have the patience to listen to me vent every day."

"Girl, I don't know how you do it. I'd be a wreck every day." Sheila hugged her. "Go, get that bath. I'll be out here."

Briana nodded, too tired to think beyond the bath and the wine. She took a sip. "I'll be out shortly."

"Take your time. I'll watch the news until you're out."

Once in the bedroom, she dropped her purse on the nightstand, fished out her cellphone and checked for any missed calls. None. Hopefully, Alejandra and Bella were settling into the shelter.

Briana knew she was too sleepy to take a long, hot bath. Instead, she opted for a quick, hot shower, more interested in the wine and propping her feet up than falling asleep in the tub. After her shower, she dried off, stepped into a pair of leggings and was pulling her T-shirt over her head when she heard a loud banging sound from the other room. She'd just stepped out of the bathroom into her bedroom when she heard Sheila scream.

Her heart raced, and her breath hitched in her chest as she ran through her bedroom. She hadn't closed the door all the way earlier. As she reached for the knob, her hand froze.

Through the crack, she saw a man wearing a ski mask, standing over Sheila's crumpled body. He had a gun in his hand with a silencer attached to the end.

Sheila lay motionless on the floor, her eyes open, red liquid pooling beneath her arm.

Please, let that be wine.

Briana's gaze went to the coffee table where Sheila's full glass of wine remained unfinished. Her heart sank.

The man nudged Sheila with his boot.

She didn't move, didn't blink her wide-open eyes. Sheila lay still as death.

Briana swallowed hard on a moan rising swiftly up her throat and backed away from the door. Looking toward the window, she shook her head. She'd never get through it without the man hearing her, and the two-story drop could lead to broken bones or death. The bathroom was out of the question. He'd look there next. With nowhere else to go, Briana grabbed her cellphone from the nightstand, dropped to the floor and slid beneath the bed. She dialed 911 and prayed for a quick response, pressing the phone to her ear.

Footsteps sounded, heading into the other bedroom, fading as he moved away.

"You've reached 911. State the nature of your emergency."

"My friend was shot," she whispered.

"Is the shooter still there?" the dispatcher asked.

The footsteps grew louder as they moved toward her bedroom.

"Yes," Briana whispered and gave her address. "Hurry, please." She ended the call, switched the phone to silent and lay still, her gaze on the door as it swung open.

Black boots and black trousers were all Briana could see of the man as he entered the room, stalked to the en suite bathroom and flung open the door.

Briana watched as he disappeared through the doorway. She heard the sound of the shower curtain rings scraping across the metal rod. The boots reappeared, coming to a stop beside her bed. The man's legs bent, and his heels came up as if he was lowering himself into a squat.

Her heart racing, Briana scooted silently across the floor toward the other side of the bed.

The faint sound of a siren wailed in the distance.

The legs straightened, and the boots carried him out of the room. A moment later, silence reigned in Briana's small apartment. She lay for a long moment, counting the seconds since she last heard the sound of footsteps.

The whole time, Briana worried about her friend Sheila. Was she still alive? Had that blood only been a superficial wound? Should she get out from under the bed and find out?

Finally, Briana rolled out from under the bed on the side farthest from the door. She crawled across the carpet and peered through the open doorway into the living room. Sheila lay where Briana had last seen her. Her eyes still open, her face pale, the blood beneath her arm making a dark stain on the white shag area rug they'd purchased together last spring.

Briana glanced toward the entry. The door to their apartment hung open, the doorframe split as if someone had kicked the door in.

Nothing moved. No footsteps sounded on the tile entry.

Still on her hands and knees, Briana crawled toward her friend, tears welling in her eyes, blurring her vision. She had to blink several times to clear them before she could reach for Sheila's neck. Pressing two fingers to the base of her throat, she waited, praying for a miracle.

No pulse. No steady rise and fall of her chest. Nothing.

"Oh, Sheila," Briana whispered, the tears falling in earnest now.

The hole in Sheila's chest told the story.

Briana sat on the floor beside her friend, holding her hand, crying.

Sirens she'd heard moments before now blared loudly outside of the apartment. Soon, several policemen entered, weapons drawn.

Briana looked to them, her heart breaking. "You're too late."

They helped her up and started the interrogation, asking questions she didn't have answers to. Her thoughts went to Alejandra and her baby, but she couldn't say a word about them without giving up their location.

When they were finished, they told her she couldn't remain there. Her apartment was now a crime scene. She would have to find another place to stay. They let her grab her purse and keys but nothing else.

"Do you need someone to drive you to a hotel?" the officer in charge asked.

She shook her head, amazed it didn't fall off as fast as it was spinning. "No," she said. "I can drive myself."

"We can provide an escort, if you'd like," he offered.

"No. I'll be all right," she said, though she knew she was lying.

Walking out of her apartment, she didn't look back. She couldn't. What had happened was inconceivable. Her mind could not comprehend it.

Briana climbed into her car and started the

engine out of sheer muscle memory. When she reached for the shift, her cellphone rang.

She dug in her purse for it and pulled it out, praying it was Sheila claiming it had all been a hoax. *Come back up to the apartment. I'm fine. Everything's fine.*

The phone didn't feel right in her hand, but nothing felt right at that moment. When she swiped her finger across the screen to answer, a voice came across, speaking a language she didn't understand. It took her a moment to realize it was Spanish. "You have the wrong number," she said and started to end the call.

The voice switched to English with a strong Spanish accent. "Who is this? Where is Alejandra?"

Briana pulled the cellphone away from her ear and stared down at it. It had a black case like hers, but the phone wasn't hers. "You will tell me where she is now," the man's voice said. "If you do not, I will find you, and I will make you tell me, if I have to beat the information out of you. Do you hear me?"

"You did this?" Briana asked. "You had my roommate killed in your effort to find Alejandra?"

"I will do whatever it takes to bring her back to El Salvador," the man's voice said.

Anger and raw hatred burned hot inside Briana, bubbling up her throat. "You can rot in hell before I tell you anything." She ended the call, lowered her window and flung the phone out onto the pavement.

"Hell, you hear me?" she yelled. Then she shifted into reverse, backed up a few feet, shifted into drive and ran over the cellphone.

The gesture wouldn't bring back Sheila, but it cut off the man who'd sent his thug to find Alejandra and who had killed her roommate in the process.

As she drove away from her apartment building, Briana knew the man wouldn't stop until he found Alejandra and her child. Briana was the only one who knew who Alejandra was and where she was staying with her daughter, Bella.

If *El Chefe Diablo* was as bad as Alejandra had indicated, he would send his killers after Briana.

She needed help. The police didn't have time to guard her, and they wouldn't do it unless she told them why *El Chefe* was after her. Briana needed someone discreet, someone she could trust implicitly. She pulled out her cellphone and dialed her brother Ryan's number. He was the only man she trusted.

"Hey, Sis," Ryan Hayes answered. "Can't talk long, I'm boarding a plane as we speak and will be out of touch for the next seventeen hours."

A sob escaped her, and she swallowed hard, trying to get words to pass her vocal cords. "Ryan."

"What's wrong," he asked, his words instantly clipped.

She couldn't speak for a full minute.

"Briana? Are you there?" he demanded. "Talk to me. Damned connection."

"I'm here," she said. "I need help."

"Oh, Bree, I'm not even in the States. What's the problem?"

"Sheila's dead," she said, her voice catching. "And I think her killer is coming for me next."

"What the fuck?" Ryan cursed. "I can't be there for another seventeen to twenty hours."

"Don't worry," she said. "I'll figure out something."

"No, wait. I know who you can call until I get back."

"Who?"

"Hank Patterson. Prior Navy SEAL. He has a security service."

"I don't know Hank."

"I have it on really good authority that he's the real deal. He and any one of his guys would lay down their lives for whomever they're protecting. I'll text you the number. Call him. No, never mind. I'll call him and have him contact you."

Briana drove down the street, away from her apartment building, not knowing where she was heading. Headlights in her rearview mirror blinded her until she shifted the mirror. "I don't know where I'll be."

"Don't worry, Bree. Get to somewhere safe. He'll figure it out," her brother said. "And Bree?"

"Yeah," she answered, on the verge of more tears.

"I love you," he said. "Stay safe. You're the only sister I have."

"I love you, too." She ended the call, turned a corner and glanced into the rearview mirror. Were those headlights the same ones that had followed her after leaving her apartment?

Increasing her speed, she rushed to the next corner and turned left, taking the turn as fast as she dared.

Again, the vehicle behind her turned and sped up.

Her heart leaped into her throat. Briana slammed her foot onto the accelerator, shooting her little car forward. She didn't slow when she took the next right turn, the rear end of her car fishtailing around the corner. Punching the gas, she raced to the next intersection where the light had just turned red. Ignoring the light, she shot through right before another car had pulled out.

The driver honked and kept moving forward, blocking the path of the vehicle following her, slowing him enough she was able to speed up and get through the next two lights and turn right then left, zigzagging through the streets until no headlights followed her.

She couldn't stay in Chicago. Briana didn't know where she could stay that would be safe. Going to a friend's house was out of the question. As Alejandra had predicted, being associated with her put others in danger. That was now true for Briana.

Briana had to find a place she could hunker down until help arrived.

ABOUT THE AUTHOR

ELLE JAMES also writing as MYLA JACKSON is a *New York Times* and *USA Today* Bestselling author of books including cowboys, intrigues and paranormal adventures that keep her readers on the edges of their seats. When she's not at her computer, she's traveling, snow skiing, boating, or riding her ATV, dreaming up new stories. Learn more about Elle James at www.ellejames.com

Website | Facebook | Twitter | GoodReads | Newsletter | BookBub | Amazon

Or visit her alter ego Myla Jackson at
mylajackson.com
Website | Facebook | Twitter | Newsletter

Follow Me!
www.ellejames.com
ellejamesauthor@gmail.com

ALSO BY ELLE JAMES

Shadow Assassin

Delta Force Strong

Ivy's Delta (Delta Force 3 Crossover)

Breaking Silence (#1)

Breaking Rules (#2)

Breaking Away (#3)

Breaking Free (#4)

Breaking Hearts (#5)

Breaking Ties (#6)

Breaking Point (#7)

Breaking Dawn (#8)

Breaking Promises (#9)

Brotherhood Protectors Yellowstone

Saving Kyla (#1)

Saving Chelsea (#2)

Saving Amanda (#3)

Saving Liliana (#4)

Saving Breely (#5)

Saving Savvie (#6)

Brotherhood Protectors Colorado

SEAL Salvation (#1)

Rocky Mountain Rescue (#2)

Ranger Redemption (#3)

Tactical Takeover (#4)

Colorado Conspiracy (#5)

Rocky Mountain Madness (#6)

Free Fall (#7)

Colorado Cold Case (#8)

Fool's Folly (#9)

Colorado Free Rein (#10)

Brotherhood Protectors

Montana SEAL (#1)

Bride Protector SEAL (#2)

Montana D-Force (#3)

Cowboy D-Force (#4)

Montana Ranger (#5)

Montana Dog Soldier (#6)

Montana SEAL Daddy (#7)

Montana Ranger's Wedding Vow (#8)

Montana SEAL Undercover Daddy (#9)

Cape Cod SEAL Rescue (#10)

Montana SEAL Friendly Fire (#11)

Montana SEAL's Mail-Order Bride (#12)

SEAL Justice (#13)

Ranger Creed (#14)

Delta Force Rescue (#15)

Dog Days of Christmas (#16)

Montana Rescue (#17)

Montana Ranger Returns (#18)

Hot SEAL Salty Dog (SEALs in Paradise)

Hot SEAL,Hawaiian Nights (SEALs in Paradise)

Hot SEAL Bachelor Party (SEALs in Paradise)

Hot SEAL, Independence Day (SEALs in Paradise)

Brotherhood Protectors Boxed Set 1

Brotherhood Protectors Boxed Set 2

Brotherhood Protectors Boxed Set 3

Brotherhood Protectors Boxed Set 4

Brotherhood Protectors Boxed Set 5

Brotherhood Protectors Boxed Set 6

Iron Horse Legacy

Soldier's Duty (#1)

Ranger's Baby (#2)

Marine's Promise (#3)

SEAL's Vow (#4)

Warrior's Resolve (#5)

Drake (#6)

Grimm (#7)

Murdock (#8)

Utah (#9)

Judge (#10)

The Outriders

Homicide at Whiskey Gulch (#1)

Hideout at Whiskey Gulch (#2)

Held Hostage at Whiskey Gulch (#3)

Setup at Whiskey Gulch (#4)

Missing Witness at Whiskey Gulch (#5)

Cowboy Justice at Whiskey Gulch (#6)

Hellfire Series

Hellfire, Texas (#1)

Justice Burning (#2)

Smoldering Desire (#3)

Hellfire in High Heels (#4)

Playing With Fire (#5)

Up in Flames (#6)

Total Meltdown (#7)

Declan's Defenders

Marine Force Recon (#1)

Show of Force (#2)

Full Force (#3)

Driving Force (#4)

Tactical Force (#5)

Disruptive Force (#6)

Mission: Six

One Intrepid SEAL

Two Dauntless Hearts

Three Courageous Words

Four Relentless Days

Five Ways to Surrender

Six Minutes to Midnight

Hearts & Heroes Series

Wyatt's War (#1)

Mack's Witness (#2)

Ronin's Return (#3)

Sam's Surrender (#4)

Take No Prisoners Series

SEAL's Honor (#1)

SEAL'S Desire (#2)

SEAL's Embrace (#3)

SEAL's Obsession (#4)

SEAL's Proposal (#5)

SEAL's Seduction (#6)

SEAL'S Defiance (#7)

SEAL's Deception (#8)

SEAL's Deliverance (#9)

SEAL's Ultimate Challenge (#10)

Texas Billionaire Club

Tarzan & Janine (#1)

Something To Talk About (#2)

Who's Your Daddy (#3)

Love & War (#4)

Billionaire Online Dating Service

The Billionaire Husband Test (#1)

The Billionaire Cinderella Test (#2)

The Billionaire Bride Test (#3)

The Billionaire Daddy Test (#4)

The Billionaire Matchmaker Test (#5)

The Billionaire Glitch Date (#6)

The Billionaire Perfect Date (#7) coming soon

The Billionaire Replacement Date (#8) coming soon

The Billionaire Wedding Date (#9) coming soon

Ballistic Cowboy

Hot Combat (#1)

Hot Target (#2)

Hot Zone (#3)

Hot Velocity (#4)

Cajun Magic Mystery Series

Voodoo on the Bayou (#1)

Voodoo for Two (#2)

Deja Voodoo (#3)

Cajun Magic Mysteries Books 1-3

SEAL Of My Own

Navy SEAL Survival

Navy SEAL Captive

Navy SEAL To Die For

Navy SEAL Six Pack

Devil's Shroud Series

Deadly Reckoning (#1)

Deadly Engagement (#2)

Deadly Liaisons (#3)

Deadly Allure (#4)

Deadly Obsession (#5)

Deadly Fall (#6)

Covert Cowboys Inc Series

Triggered (#1)

Taking Aim (#2)

Bodyguard Under Fire (#3)

Cowboy Resurrected (#4)

Navy SEAL Justice (#5)

Navy SEAL Newlywed (#6)

High Country Hideout (#7)

Clandestine Christmas (#8)

Thunder Horse Series

Hostage to Thunder Horse (#1)

Thunder Horse Heritage (#2)

Thunder Horse Redemption (#3)

Christmas at Thunder Horse Ranch (#4)

Demon Series

Hot Demon Nights (#1)

Demon's Embrace (#2)

Tempting the Demon (#3)

Lords of the Underworld

Witch's Initiation (#1)

Witch's Seduction (#2)

The Witch's Desire (#3)

Possessing the Witch (#4)

Stealth Operations Specialists (SOS)

Nick of Time

Alaskan Fantasy

Blown Away

Warrior's Conquest

Enslaved by the Viking Short Story

Conquests

Smokin' Hot Firemen

Protecting the Colton Bride

Protecting the Colton Bride & Colton's Cowboy Code

Heir to Murder

Secret Service Rescue

High Octane Heroes

Haunted

Engaged with the Boss

Cowboy Brigade

Time Raiders: The Whisper

Bundle of Trouble

Killer Body